A HOME WITH AUNT FLORRY

A HOME WITH AUNT FLORRY

Charlene Joy Talbot

Atheneum 1974 New York

Frontispiece by Gail Owens

Library of Congress Cataloging in Publication Data
Talbot, Charlene Joy.
   A home with Aunt Florry.
   SUMMARY: When orphaned twins Wendy and
Jason go to New York to live with their bohemian
aunt, they find her life quite different from what they
had known in Kansas.
   [1. Orphans—Fiction. 2. New York (City)—
Fiction] I. Title.
PZ7.T1418Ho   [Fic]   74-75572
ISBN 0-689-30440-4

Library of Congress catalog card number 74-75572
ISBN 0-689-30440-4
Published simultaneously in Canada by
McClelland & Stewart, Ltd.
Manufactured in the United States of America
by Quinn & Boden Company, Inc.
Rahway, New Jersey
First Edition

To my mother

Contents

A HOME WITH
AUNT FLORRY

Three Travelers

BY THE TIME THE TWINS AND AUNT FLORRY ARRIVED at the airport, the reception area was crowded with people also flying to New York. But Aunt Florry seemed to know what to do. She pushed up to a man standing behind a desk and shoved their tickets at him. He pasted something on each and waved them to where the crowd was thickest, where you gave your hand baggage to uniformed people behind a table and lined up to walk through an arch.

"The weapons check, children," Aunt Florry said in her loud voice. "So we won't get hijacked."

The twins watched a carefully dressed blue-haired woman walk through the arch. A buzzer snarled.

"Jason!" Wendy gasped. "Has she got a gun?"

"No! That man's taking her glasses. I think the chain on her glasses made it go off."

The guard directed the woman to go through again. The buzzer was silent—mollified. The guard gave back the glasses, and the woman picked up her handbag and disappeared down the corridor.

When Aunt Florry's turn came, she plunked down two bags stuffed full of last-minute things, including crackers and cheese spread. It was amazing that she had been able to find their tickets. Jason was so busy watching the man go through Aunt Florry's accumulation, to make sure she wasn't carrying a gun, that he forgot to point out to the next checker that his neat plaid bag was a cat carrier. The air hostess flopped the bag on its side and unzipped it. Elf, Jason's orange Persian, raised up and looked around, insulted.

The hostess let out a shriek. Heads turned. "I didn't know it was a cat!" she exclaimed, seeking sympathy.

Jason, in line to go through the arch, pretended the cat wasn't his. Wendy poked him and giggled.

The uniformed man took over and zipped Elf back into her carrier. She was set gently at the end of the table. Jason walked through the arch. The buzzer didn't object.

Aunt Florry, waiting on the other side, hadn't seen what happened. Jason was glad of that. He hadn't known her long, but he knew she would have fussed at the woman for her stupidity—flopping a cat on its side, and then screaming at it. Still embarrassed, he retrieved Elf's carrier. Wendy came through the arch and picked up her shoulder bag. Then they went through a tunnel and onto the plane.

Their seats were in the first row behind the partition. Wendy took the window seat, but she offered to change with him halfway. Jason sat on the aisle, and set the carrier at his feet. He stretched his neck to take a last look at Kansas, and then settled back to listen to Aunt Florry, sitting between them. She was talking about where they were going to live.

". . . with lots of space. You know, space is very scarce in New York. Children often have to share their bedrooms."

"Who with?" Jason visualized a succession of strangers, with suitcases . . . like a hotel.

"With brothers and sisters! But where we're going, you'll have a whole floor to yourselves . . . and windows on *two* sides, with wide windowsills for plants, if you like."

Jason remembered a big one-room cabin where they had stayed once in Colorado. Well, it had actually had a small bedroom on either end, but the one big room had been living room, dining room, and kitchen. The cabin was backed against a hillside, so the only windows were across the front. When you looked out, all you could see was green—green—green. His mother had said it gave her the willies.

The thought of his mother made him aware of the ache in his chest. The ache was there all the time, but sometimes now he could shove it beneath the surface of his thoughts so that he didn't notice it for a while. He made an effort to do so again.

Maybe Aunt Florry's place was something like that cabin. No—New York was a city.

He asked, "Are there any kids in the neighborhood?"

"There's one boy—about your age."

Wendy began listening, too, leaning forward against her seat belt. "Will we have bedrooms of our own?"

"*You* may, if you like," Aunt Florry said. "There's a little room at one end."

That made Aunt Florry's house sound like the cabin again. Perhaps, Jason thought, it's on the side of a hill in the city.

"Do you have a room?" Wendy asked.

Aunt Florry laughed. "Yes, yes. I have the whole floor above you . . . and the one above that!"

Jason shook his head, as though to shake away the idea of the cabin. It must be a very big house. Plainly Aunt Florry liked it.

"Why does it only have windows on two sides?"

"Because other buildings are built up against it."

When lunch was over and the hostess had taken away the trays, Jason put his head back and closed his eyes. He tried to imagine a house three-stories high with windows on only two sides. It sounded like the buildings on Main Street. Some of those had apartments upstairs. They looked hot and dark. Would Aunt Florry's place be like that?

His heart thudded. What if he and Wendy didn't like it?

He thought about that for a while and felt frightened. Because what could they do if they didn't like it? Everything had happened so fast—the accident, then Aunt Florry (whom they scarcely knew) arriving, then the funeral, and then a lot of talk behind closed doors, and Dad's lawyer asking how they would like to live with Aunt Florry in New York. Jason had known there wasn't really any choice—the lawyer thought that was the best thing for them. So here they were.

Oh, it would surely be all right. Aunt Florry wasn't an editor like his father, but she was some kind of writer, and she was, after all, their aunt. So she couldn't be mean to them. And living in the city should be, at least, *interesting*.

He knew there was plenty of money, so they wouldn't be poor, or anything. Aunt Florry had inherited half of Grandpa's publishing company years ago, and Dad had inherited half, and now Dad's half belonged to him and Wendy. He wished he didn't feel so scared. He looked at his sister. She didn't look worried.

What would it be like not to have any front yard

—or backyard, either? Where would Goblin stay? There must be a backyard. Unless Aunt Florry meant for the dog to live in the house. Goblin would like that!

Wendy had already pictured her new home to herself. She hoped it would be near the park, because across from the park was where the dinosaurs were. It said so in a book, and her best friend had been there. Wendy couldn't wait to see them. Imagine getting to dig up old bones. She meditated on the cow's skull packed among her clothes. She had found it in a pasture. There hadn't been any backbones to go with it, but it might be old. She hoped it was packed okay.

And Morgan—she hoped Morgan was okay, somewhere in the bowels of the plane. You could take only one pet with you in the cabin, and poor Morgan la Fay had had to go with the baggage.

She considered asking about the museum, but Aunt Florry looked asleep. There would be time.

Instead, she imagined again a big house, three-stories high, on a corner, with a small yard on the front and side, and the houses so close on the other side and rear that windows were not worthwhile. You could only look into your neighbor's window. That might be fun, if you had a friend. You could climb into each other's bedrooms. It would be like living in the same house, only with windows instead of doors.

Aunt Florry sat with her eyes closed and thought pleasantly of her building. She imagined how a passerby might see it, how she would see it when she arrived. Big windows giving a clear glimpse of buxom, self-assured plants, the room-sized palm tree grown from a date seed, pink and red geraniums on the fire escape, and pigeons flashing and wheeling above the roof. The passerby would see paintings hanging on the walls, and bookshelves floor to ceiling (as soon as she got around to building them). If he looked at her tenant's windows on the second floor, he would see canvases in the process of being painted. And, of course, on the ground floor the wholesale butter-and-egg business.

The discerning passerby would know that someone bohemian and creative lived there. It was a far cry from Kansas; it was to make herself this kind of home that she had come to New York fifteen years ago. There was no reason why two children should not fit in.

Jason and Wendy

NEW YORK CITY WAS STEAMY THAT AFTERNOON. Tomas Lorca sat on a loading dock watching a trailer van trying to back against the dock across the street. The cab had to be parked at right angles to the trailer or the whole street would be blocked. As it was, a line of cars and trucks was waiting while the driver struggled. Soon someone would begin to honk.

The trucker settled his truck at last and climbed down from the cab, mopping his face. Traffic began to move.

At the end of the line came a yellow taxicab. But instead of going on past, it stopped. And out of it climbed Tomas's gray-haired, sturdy neighbor, Miss Florry Ward. Tomas had not seen her for more than a week. She had gone to Kansas to bring back her niece and nephew. They were there, too. The boy was getting out on the street side. Florry yelled at him, but he was already out.

He was tall, his longish hair was light brown, and he held what looked like a cat carrier. The girl got out onto the sidewalk. She was tall, also. They were twelve, Florry had told Tomas. And twins. The girl had something live in a wooden box that she was speaking to.

Tomas heard Florry talking steadily. Telling the driver to be careful as he took three suitcases out of the trunk, telling him to set them on the sidewalk, telling the boy he must never get out on the street side of taxis, telling the girl to watch the suitcases while she paid the fare.

The two kids looked around at the trucks and the four-and-five-story-buildings. Florry crossed the sidewalk to her door. Unlike the front door of Tomas's building down the block, no steps led up to this one, and no glass allowed one to look inside.

Florry opened her pocketbook to get her keys, surveying the neighborhood while she felt for them, and with that she saw Tomas.

"Tomas! Hello!" she shouted. "Come and meet my lovely niece and nephew. Children!" Tomas slid off the loading dock and moved forward. The boy and girl came to stand beside Florry, looking very lost.

"I want you to meet your neighbor, Tomas Lorca. Tomas, this is my niece, Wendy, and my nephew,

Jason. Tomas is thirteen. He's an orphan, too," she explained.

The boy turned away. Tears came into the girl's eyes. And Tomas remembered what he had known for a long time: Florry Ward had the biggest mouth in the neighborhood. Mrs. Malloy had said so more than once.

The boy said, "Hi," and then he said, "Aunt Florry, this isn't your *house*, is it? This is a store."

"It's a butter-and-egg business on the first floor, but above, it's my house." She threw her head back and looked proudly up at it, though they were all standing too close to see anything but the fire escape winding upward in a confusion of ladders and railings.

The twins looked at each other. Some message seemed to pass between them.

"It's probably very nice *inside*," Wendy said stoutly.

Tomas felt she was in for a surprise.

The twins looked very tanned. In fact, their skin was almost the color of their hair. They must have been to the beach a lot, Tomas decided. Then he remembered there were no beaches in Kansas.

"What's in the box?" Tomas asked Jason. Florry was still hunting for keys.

"My cat," Jason said.

"And this is my rat." Wendy held up her box.

"You brought a rat from Kansas?" Tomas asked in astonishment.

"A *white* rat," Florry explained. She obviously knew what Tomas was thinking: the neighborhood had enough rats already. "Oh, those blessed keys," she went on. "I know they're here—ah, yes!"

Aunt Florry said, "Children, put your pets inside the door. This door must always be locked. Tomas—"

Tomas began moving away. "See you later!" he called. He knew Florry. She was always getting him to work for her. Some days he didn't mind. She was fun to listen to. But today was too hot. He remembered there might be cold soda in Mrs. Malloy's refrigerator.

Jason and Wendy lugged their suitcases across the sidewalk and set them in the entryway. From there they caught a glimpse of gray, dusty stairs. They moved their possessions inside; Aunt Florry locked the door behind them and they were in semidarkness.

"This door must always be locked," she repeated. "I'll give you each a key. You must lock it every time you go out, and from the inside every time you come in. For that you don't need a key. Just turn this knob. Clockwise."

"But this isn't a house, Aunt Florry!" Wendy objected.

"Certainly not. It's a commercial building. Tsk! The bulb's out. No wonder it's dark. Well, go on up, but be careful. Did you each take a suitcase?"

"No—" Jason said, from halfway up the first flight.

"Me, neither," Wendy announced, just behind him.

"Children!" Aunt Florry exclaimed. "You must learn to wait on yourselves! Who is going to bring them up if you don't?"

"We'll get them later," Jason mumbled. He wanted a drink of water. And he wanted to see what kind of crazy place Aunt Florry had brought them to. In the back of his mind was the feeling that he and Wendy wouldn't really *be* here if they didn't bring their suitcases up.

He reached the top of the long flight. A dirty window there looked out on a wall. A kind of gloomy twilight came through and showed the dusty hall that ran beside the stairs to the foot of the next flight.

"Where to now?" he asked.

"Up one more," Aunt Florry said. "This is Luke Harrison's floor. He's my tenant."

They proceeded up another flight. Grimy windows at each end of the hallway gave light enough to see by.

"Right here," Aunt Florry said. "This is your door."

Jason reached out to open it.

"No—no! It's locked," Aunt Florry said, as though he were stupid. "Just a minute." She began hunting for the right key on the bunch. "I'm going to let you children have this whole floor. It was lucky—the couple who lived here decided to move not long before I got that terrible phone call about your parents." She found the key and turned it in the lock. "There—"

She flung open the door like a fairy godmother bestowing a castle.

Jason and Wendy beheld a room, larger and more cheerless than a three-car garage. Windows on two sides gave plenty of light, showing a vast, bare space, empty except for a potbellied stove and a sink.

The twins were speechless, stunned.

Aunt Florry seemed to sense their dismay for she began to talk very fast: "It's called a loft. In the old days it was used for light manufacturing. But that's all over. Now people live in them—Everyone who can afford it. So much more room—Artists and people on the fringe of the arts. Go in! Go in!"

Jason and Wendy stepped inside. Jason set the cat carrier down and opened it. Elf stepped cautiously out and looked around with as much bewilderment as her master.

"Don't artists have furniture?" Wendy said in a small voice.

"Of course they have furniture!" Aunt Florry exclaimed. "Oh! You mean here! Your own furniture will be here in a day or so."

She was right, Jason realized. So many things had happened so fast, like something in the middle of the night, and next morning you didn't remember until someone reminded you. Aunt Florry had arranged to have his and Wendy's bedroom furniture sent to New York. They would have that much of home. Everything else was going to be sold . . . even the house. They could not go back.

Aunt Florry started around the big room, opening windows.

Jason went to the sink. His footsteps sounded hollow crossing the room.

"Let the water run," Aunt Florry cried. "It hasn't been used all month." Her voice sounded echo-y, too.

Wendy set Morgan la Fay's box on the floor, but she didn't open it. The nearest wall had a door in it. "Where does that go?" she asked suspiciously.

"Take a look," Aunt Florry encouraged. "That's the room I thought you might like."

Wendy opened the door to a bare space with one window overlooking the street.

"This was the office," Aunt Florry explained. "I think this floor was used for a printshop."

Leaving the water to run, Jason went to peer over their shoulders. "Printing?" He cast a professional eye about the loft. "I guess it would make a good job pressroom."

"Yeah?" Wendy objected. "How would you get the paper in?"

"There's an old freight elevator," Aunt Florry said, taking them into a dark corner between the office and the door to the hall.

Aunt Florry had brought up the one subject— printing—that could make the twins feel less bewildered, for they came from a newspaper family. Their grandfather had founded a paper in Kansas. Aunt Florry and their father had grown up to the smell of printer's ink, and so had the twins. The big presses at the newspaper building rolled out a morning and an evening paper, and a number of monthly farm papers.

So it was possible for Jason to imagine living in an empty pressroom, though it was the craziest thing he'd ever heard of.

Florry opened a door and showed them an elevator shaft behind a wooden grille.

"Does it work?" Wendy asked.

"When necessary. It's not a plaything."

"We can bring up our suitcases with it!" Jason exclaimed, and then wished he hadn't said it. He had somehow committed himself and Wendy to staying. Though of course they had to, anyway.

"Yes, yes! The very thing!" Aunt Florry agreed, adding, "Jason, the water has run long enough."

He plodded back to the sink.

Aunt Florry pointed to the little room. "If I were you, Wendy dear, I would make this my bedroom."

"What about Jason?"

"Pooh!" Aunt Florry said. "Boys don't need bedrooms. He can choose any corner out here that he wants."

They followed him to the sink. He had found a glass and was drinking deeply.

"What's this?" Wendy asked, seeing another walled-off corner. "Oh!" She read the old tin sign that said GENTLEMEN and stepped back from the door.

"Don't let a silly sign stop you!" Aunt Florry scoffed. "This is your bathroom." She opened the door and Wendy peered in. She saw a stall shower, another sink, and a toilet.

"Wen—want a drink?" Jason handed her a glass. She looked at it with a frown. It wasn't the cleanest glass she had ever seen, but she was too thirsty to be particular.

"Elf wants a drink, too," she said, but at that moment the wispy Persian leaped to the rim of the sink and began lapping water from the tap.

"I'll give you some dishes for her," Aunt Florry told Jason. "Of course, you'll both eat upstairs with me. But isn't this a lovely space? You can sleep here and study here, and you'll have so much room to run around in."

Try as he would, Jason could think of nothing to say. He wanted to be polite, and if Aunt Florry said this was a place to live, he guessed it must be, but all he could feel was terribly lonely. It would be better, he hoped, when Goblin arrived, and the beds and the rest of their stuff.

"Where are we going to sleep till our beds come?" he asked.

Aunt Florry waved a hand. "We'll fix something. I

have two perfectly good mattresses we can bring down. It'll only be for a night or two."

Wendy was looking out the window at the building across the street. "Those people can see right into my bedroom."

Aunt Florry made a face. "They only work there. They can't see in unless you turn the lights on. By that time they'll be gone home."

"Home—" Wendy looked around the big bare room, and her eyes filled with tears. She turned back toward the windows.

"My dear—" Aunt Florry started to put out a hand and then cocked her head. "My telephone!" she cried and ran from the room. Somewhere above their heads, Jason could hear a phone ringing.

"I want to go home, too!" Wendy sank down on the wide windowsill and began to cry in earnest.

Jason, still feeling curiously unreal, went over to pat her shoulder. "Aw, come on, Wendy. Stop it. She'll give you curtains if you want them."

"It's not curtains," Wendy sobbed. "It's the whole place. It's *horrible!* I thought we were going to a house!"

"It's crazy," Jason admitted. "But maybe it won't be too bad," he said cautiously. "I don't think she'll care how much noise we make, or how late we stay up. She won't even know."

Wendy lifted her head and looked around the room.

Then with a howl she jumped to her feet, brushing the back of her skirt. Her fingers had come in contact with a film of grit on the windowsill. "Look! It's *dirty,* too!" she wept.

"Well, you can't go home!" Jason shouted. "There isn't any."

Wendy gulped and stopped crying. She took a handkerchief from her pocket and blew her nose. "I know. I'm sorry."

"You don't have to be sorry. I feel like crying, too, half the time."

Wendy looked at him, her blue eyes wide. "You never do," she said.

"Not when anyone's watching," Jason mumbled.

Wendy looked thoughtful.

Jason said, "You know—one thing—I think we get to keep Goblin in here, too. Where else is there?"

"Jason," Wendy said slowly, "do you think everybody in New York lives like this?"

"No. You heard her say. Artists and people like that. In all those TV shows everybody lives in huge apartments."

"Listen. I think she's coming back," Wendy whispered.

Aunt Florry

THEY HEARD FOOTSTEPS OUTSIDE IN THE HALL, AND then Aunt Florry appeared in the doorway. She was holding a saucer in one hand. "Oh! That telephone!" she cried. "No sooner do I get in the house— That was the delivery people about the dog. They've just picked him up at the airport and are bringing him now. They called to make sure someone would be here."

"Poor Goblin," Jason said. "He's been in that box since this morning."

"Aunt Florry, do we get to keep him in here?" Wendy asked.

"Oh my, yes. Where else could you keep him? He's housebroken, isn't he?"

The twins nodded, not looking at each other for fear of showing how pleased they were.

"You'll have to walk him, of course—night and

21

morning," Aunt Florry was saying. "It will be good exercise for all of you." She started for the door. "Come! I want to show you the rest of the place."

Jason and Wendy started to follow her, but on passing the little box that held Morgan la Fay, she stopped. "Wendy! Don't let me forget to find the cage I promised you. Did you give her water?"

"I need a saucer," Wendy explained.

Aunt Florry let out a shriek of laughter that made Jason and Wendy both jump.

"Ha!" she cried. "Here!" She held out the saucer. "I forgot I had it in my hand. Ha-ha-ha! I'm losing my mind!"

Jason didn't know whether to laugh or not, so he smiled politely.

Wendy filled the saucer at the sink, then unfastened the lid of the box. "Here, Morgan, my precious," she purred. She held the rat gently in one corner while she set the saucer in the other. "Only be patient a while longer. Soon you shall have a new cage." As she closed the box, the rat was twitching its whiskers over the water.

They proceeded out into the hall, climbed another flight of dusty stairs, and entered another door exactly like their own. The room was the same size as theirs, but the resemblance stopped there.

"This is my floor," Aunt Florry said. "See how it fills up with a little furniture?"

Any room would fill up if it held that much furniture! Jason thought. There was so much, there was only an aisle through it. The aisle led to a little cleared space by the sink. The sink, the stove, and the refrigerator looked as though they had backed against the wall in terror of the rising tide of objects. A few feet away from them a large table, every inch of its surface covered with small items, seemed to be trying to shoulder back the clutter.

Aunt Florry began chattering about supper.

Jason studied the tabletop. It looked like one of those tests they give to improve people's powers of observation: *Study this assortment for 30 seconds and list the objects you can remember.*

Jason looked at the floor and began saying to himself: sugar bowl, newspaper, fork, cup, cracker box, hammer, dust (was it fair to count dust?), dried apple, stack of books, small wooden cheesebox, jar of something, lots of jars, actually, and some were empty . . .

"Oh! It's just *so* dirty," Aunt Florry was saying. "And of course I left in such a rush. The minute you're gone for a week, the place just falls apart."

It didn't look to Jason as if it could have gotten that way just by Aunt Florry rushing to leave for Kansas.

Wendy was ominously silent.

"What time is it?" Aunt Florry studied a greasy-looking plastic clock above the stove. "Only three o'clock. That's all right. I must get to the store, but we'll wait for Goblin. He'll want some exercise. I hope you both know how to do dishes."

Jason nodded. Wendy said, "We did them once for a week when the dishwasher broke. Mother made Jason help, too."

"I'm glad to hear that!" Aunt Florry said.

"It's nice to have a dishwasher, though," Wendy told her.

"Ugh!" Aunt Florry said. "So middle class!"

Jason was thinking that if it would only bring back his mother, he'd do the dishes every day. Gladly. He opened his eyes very wide, hoping that the mist that filled them wouldn't run over into tears.

"This place is a mess," Aunt Florry announced. "You children can help clean it tomorrow. Or the next day. We must get to it soon."

Wendy said, "Ugh!" very clearly, but either Aunt Florry didn't hear, or she pretended not to.

"And now for the surprise!" Aunt Florry cried. "This way." She led them back down the aisle to the door. "I have pets, too. On up, one more flight. Jason, I think, will be particularly intrigued."

Wendy nudged him at that, and he turned to look at her. She was grinning.

Aunt Florry paused before the door on the next floor. She opened it with great ceremony. Jason and

Wendy peered over her shoulders, ready to expect anything. The near half of the room was stacked with more furniture, but halfway down the room a chicken-wire screen stretched from floor to ceiling. Behind it Jason saw pigeons—walking about, cooing to themselves. Others were roosting on wide shelves along the wall.

Aunt Florry rushed at the chicken-wire door. "Here, pidgie, pidgie, pidgie! How are you, my darlings, my fine, feathered friends?"

The loft broke into noise and movement. Flapping, fluttering, swooping birds churned the dusty air. They filled the whole space with their wings, flashing now gray, now silver in the light from the windows.

"Look! Look!" Aunt Florry cried. "Oh, they're so glad to see me!" She scooped a handful of grain from a bag near the door.

"Stay where you are," she told the twins unnecessarily. Unlatching the screen door she went in, closing it quickly behind her. The pigeons landed on her shoulders, her head, her arms, and on each other in the friendliest way possible, pecking at the feed in her hand as often as they could crowd up to it. One tangled its feet in her curly gray hair.

"Ouch!" she shouted, laughing and waving it away. "Hello, my darlings, did you miss me? Are you glad to see me?"

Apparently they were. They ate all the grain in her hand and kept coming back, looking for more.

"Was Luke good to you?" the twins heard her ask above the noise of flapping wings. She made her way to the sink. "I see you have lots of nice clean drinky."

"Drinky!" Jason muttered.

"I'll bet he didn't let you out today. You shall stretch your wings, now. We'll go up on the roof and see them fly," she yelled back at Wendy and Jason.

She opened a window in the wall opposite the street. One by one the birds hurled themselves out except a few who seemed to be sitting on nests. The loft was suddenly quiet.

Aunt Florry came back to the twins, after closing the chicken-wire door.

"Well?" she asked, smiling.

"Are they yours?" Wendy gasped.

Aunt Florry looked pleased. "Yes. At last count I had 207. All from a mama and papa bird who were raising two babies on that window ledge." She pointed to the open window.

"Did you tame them?" Jason asked, interested in spite of himself. He had decided he was *not* going to be intrigued, no matter what Aunt Florry had to show him.

"I lured them inside with some grain," Aunt Florry explained. "The young ones grew up tame. I let them out only once a day to fly. They soon got used to it.

Luckily they were male and female. All our city pigeons came from once-tame doves that escaped, so it's easy to retame them. If they're sheltered, they raise seven or eight broods a year, so you can see that in four years I have a lot of feathered friends."

"Come," she said, shooing them into the hall. "If you ever feed the pigeons, you must make sure to keep this door closed."

"Why?" Jason asked.

"Because nothing must get at them, or disturb them. Goblin, for instance, or Elf."

"Goblin wouldn't!" Wendy exclaimed.

"He's a hunting dog, isn't he?" Aunt Florry insisted. "And think what fun a cat could have! Here, let me go first!"

Her bossiness annoyed Jason. Following her up the steps, he said, "Pigeons get disturbed in the park, don't they?"

"Those are different," she stated. "These are pets. They've been secluded."

She reached the top of the stairs, unhooked the roof door, and stepped out into the sunshine. "Look! Children! Look! Look!" she cried, pointing up.

Jason and Wendy looked.

Overhead the birds were flying in a circle, wheeling as a flock, moving and turning all at the same time, like a bouquet of birds being swung round and round on a long string.

"How do you know they won't fly off?" Wendy asked.

"This is their home," Aunt Florry replied. "Where would they go?"

Like us, Jason thought. Where could we go?

He turned his attention to the view. Nearby nothing was to be seen but rooftops. A few blocks away the buildings began to get higher, blocking the sky. Not a treetop could he see. Aunt Florry's was a corner building. To the west and north the walls of the buildings next door rose above the roof they were on.

"Where's the park?" Wendy asked. "The one with the museum?"

"Oh, that's way uptown." Aunt Florry dismissed it with a look of disgust. "You don't want to go up there!"

Jason wondered why Wendy looked furious. How come she wanted a park?

A low wide wall prevented him from peering down into the street. He was about to climb up on it when he remembered he was wearing good clothes, and everything he touched felt gritty. His hands were quite black.

Aunt Florry was explaining to Wendy that the ropes stretched haphazardly across the roof were clotheslines. "We'll hang the wash up here on nice days," she said.

Jason thought, Poor Wendy, she'll have to help.

Aunt Florry stayed watching the pigeons.

"How do you get them back in?" Jason asked.

Wendy said, "I already know. They go back by themselves. When they're tired."

"How long before they get tired?" Jason asked. It was hot on the roof. He wanted to take off his good pants and put on shorts. And go barefoot, too.

"Auntie?" With the same thought Wendy went straight to the point. "Can I put on shorts?"

"Of course you can! You don't have to ask me! Oh! I forgot you're wearing good clothes. Why, so am I! Yes, yes. We must do that next." She started down the stairs.

The twins followed.

"Hook the door!" she called over her shoulder. "Change clothes and come back up. I'll show you the furniture. You can pick what you need for tonight. Chairs to put your clothes on, and—"

"We usually hang them up," Wendy interrupted.

Aunt Florry paused at her door. "Certainly! Certainly! Find the closet! It's across from the elevator."

She went into her room. The twins went sedately downstairs. Opening their door, they were astonished again at the size and emptiness of the place.

Elf jumped down from a windowsill and came mewing to greet them.

"Jason," Wendy said, "do you think Daddy knew

she didn't live in a house, or an apartment, or something? Did he ever visit her?"

Jason frowned, trying to remember. "Maybe—before we were born. He wrote to her pretty often. He tried to coax her to go to Colorado with us one year—remember? But she didn't."

"Maybe he thought we'd like it here."

Jason stared at her. "Are you kidding?"

He looked around for his clothes and realized their suitcases were still downstairs.

"Aunt Florry forgot to show us how to use the elevator. I'm going to bring my suitcase up the stairs."

"Mine's too heavy," Wendy objected.

"Come on! Do you want to change clothes or don't you?"

They went down to where the suitcases waited. Jason picked out his.

"Here's mine," Wendy said. "Jason, it's *so* heavy!"

Jason hefted it. "It is not! Don't be so helpless. You'd better learn to look after yourself. I don't think Aunt Florry's going to do it."

"I do look after myself," Wendy pouted. At any rate, she did pick up her suitcase and carry it upstairs to her "room" though not without cries of pain and effort.

Jason found his shorts and removed his long pants with a sigh of comfort. He put them back in the suitcase. There was no place else, everything was so dusty.

It's like camping, he thought, only there the ground is cleaner.

"My skull's okay," Wendy shouted to him.

She came out carrying her dress. She opened one of the closet doors and found a hanger. "Look, Jason," she said. "The closet's in two parts. Look how big it is! You can have one side, and I'll have the other."

"Okay," Jason said. "Come on."

They found Aunt Florry wearing faded blue jeans torn off below the knees, a short-sleeved plaid shirt, and sneakers. Her short gray hair stood on end. Now that she was no longer wearing shoes with heels, Jason discovered that he was as tall as she. So was Wendy.

The furniture she wanted them to take was all jumbled together in the near half of the pigeons' loft. She had to remove several things before Jason and Wendy could get at the two chairs and the mattresses she had chosen for them. She also gave them each a coatrack to hang things on.

By the time they had carried it all downstairs, it was four o'clock. And Goblin had not come.

"What if they can't find the place?" Jason said, worried.

"How can they not find the place?" Aunt Florry demanded, and his fear subsided.

"I'll bet he'll be thirsty," he said.

"I'm sure he'll be glad to get out," Aunt Florry said.

At that moment the doorbell rang.

"That's him!" Jason shouted. "Wendy! Come on!"

The twins pelted down the stairs, and Aunt Florry hurried in their wake.

"I'll need my purse," she cried.

Outside the downstairs door, a man holding a piece of paper said, "Ward?"

"Yes," Jason said. Wendy nodded breathlessly.

"Got a dog here," the man said. "Fifteen dollars."

Aunt Florry came down in time to hear him.

"Fifteen dollars!" she cried. "Why, they deliver *people* from the airport for less than that."

"Yes, ma'am," the driver said. "People don't have to be carried in and out of trucks."

The twins giggled.

Aunt Florry said, "I suppose you're right." She counted out three bills. "Here. You're sure it's the right dog?"

"The box says Ward," the driver told her, "and this is the address, but you can look for yourselves."

He crossed to the van parked at the curb, and he and his helper slung the crate to the ground. Goblin, catching sight of his family through the steel mesh, let out a yap of recognition.

"That's our Goblin," Wendy said.

"Okay, Miss," the driver said. "Sign here, please." He laid the bill on top of the box, handed Wendy his pencil, and pointed to a line. She wrote her name carefully.

He took the paper, climbed into his truck, and drove away.

"Poor boy," Jason soothed the dog. "Did you have a nice trip? I'll have you out in a minute."

"Don't let him loose on the street," Aunt Florry cautioned.

Jason said, "No, I won't. Here, Wendy, hold up the door while I get hold of his collar."

The setter came out, panting with happiness at seeing his owners, and he began wagging his tail so hard that his whole red-brown back shook.

"Come on, boy. Come on upstairs."

"We can't leave the box on the sidewalk," Aunt Florry said. "Wendy, you take Goblin upstairs. Jason, stay here with the box. Wendy and I will bring the elevator down. We can take up the box and my suitcase."

So Jason sat out on the box and waited. He looked up and down the street. Most of the trucks were gone now. The streets were empty, except for a few people walking past, and yet for some reason he felt scared. He hoped Aunt Florry would hurry.

He heard machinery running and looked toward the building. A big door he hadn't noticed began to open. One half slid up, the other down. Wendy and

Aunt Florry appeared in the opening. It was just like the freight elevators at the printing plant.

"Isn't it great!" Wendy exclaimed.

"Put the box in," Aunt Florry directed, "and then get the rest of the suitcases."

Wendy helped carry the box without being asked. She even helped with the suitcases.

"Lock the stair door, and we'll ride up," Aunt Florry said, giving Jason the key.

It wasn't much of a ride, but it did deliver all the heavy things to their floor.

The water dish inside Goblin's crate was empty, and he was thirsty. Wendy and Jason filled the dish three times before the dog had enough.

"All right, children, hurry now, before the store closes. Where's Goblin's leash?"

"In my bag," Wendy said. She found her bag on the floor next to her suitcase, put the leash on Goblin, and they set out, Jason leading Goblin, or rather, Goblin leading Jason, and Aunt Florry hauling a battered, wire shopping cart.

"Goblin's not used to a leash," Wendy explained.

"He'll have to get used to it," Aunt Florry said. "All New York dogs go on leashes. You wouldn't want him to get frightened and run off."

"No," Wendy agreed. "Poor Goblin, you're going to be a city dog."

"Now, let's see." Aunt Florry laughed her hearty

laugh. "We need dog food, cat food, and people food. What about rat food?"

"Morgan eats anything," Wendy bragged. "She's very good about eating leftovers."

They walked several blocks to the store. The buildings seemed to go on forever in every direction. "Is all New York like this?" Jason asked. "All buildings?"

"Oh, yes," Aunt Florry said. "All the island of Manhattan, at any rate. There are parks, of course, but no houses with front yards." C821642 CO. SCHOOLS

The store was the smallest they had ever seen. Everything was packed tightly on small shelves, set in only two aisles. Every spare bit of space had its own set of shelves. Jason waited outside with Goblin, who didn't know what to make of it all. The dog turned this way and that, looking at every passing person, but was too nervous to sit down or take an interest in smelling things.

"Take it easy, old boy," Jason said, patting him. "You'll get used to it. I guess."

Jason pulled the cart home, and Wendy held Goblin.

"How come you don't have a car, Aunt Florry?" Jason asked. Shopping had been much easier in Shawnee City.

"Where would I keep it?" she asked. "A car's nothing but a nuisance in the city."

"You could carry groceries in it."

"Nonsense!" Aunt Florry said. "It doesn't hurt to

walk a few blocks with groceries. You and Wendy don't have your bicycles. You'll be needing exercise."

Wendy gave Jason a suffering look, which annoyed him. After all, she wasn't hauling the groceries.

They took the freight elevator to Aunt Florry's floor. As soon as they stepped into the room, she shrieked and laughed because Goblin couldn't turn around without hitting something with his feathery tail.

"Take him downstairs," she cried. "You'll have to keep him downstairs until we get this place straightened up. Better yet—take him outside and walk him some more while I start supper."

"Okay. Come on, Wendy," Jason said.

"The key!" Aunt Florry screeched as they were leaving the room. "You're forgetting you have to lock the door."

Wendy ran back for it.

"We must get copies made tomorrow," Aunt Florry said.

"Yes, Aunt Florry. I'll remember," Wendy promised.

It would be rather grown-up to have your own house key.

Tomas

WENDY LOCKED THE DOWNSTAIRS DOOR BEHIND THEM, and they stood on the sidewalk wondering which way to walk. Jason held very tight to Goblin's leash.

"We better not get lost," Wendy said.

Jason saw Tomas Lorca standing in the doorway of his building at the other end of the block. He was wearing a red-and-white striped T-shirt that looked too big for him, cut-off jeans, and rubber thong sandals.

"Let's go this way," Jason said, starting toward him.

"He looks Mexican," Wendy said under her breath.

"Puerto Rican," Jason said. "There are no Mexicans in New York."

"How do you know?" Wendy demanded, but before Jason could answer they were within speaking distance of Tomas.

"Hi," Jason said.

"You have a dog, too?" Tomas asked, backing away as Goblin went toward him, tail wagging, to give him a friendly sniff.

"He won't bite," Jason said, hauling Goblin back.

"He never bites anybody," Wendy said. Both boys looked at her because she sounded a little sorry.

Tomas said, "I had a friend once who had a dog. I used to walk it for her. It was little, though. This one must eat a lot."

"Yeah," Jason said agreeably. The dog food arrived from the store in a big bag. When it was empty, another bag arrived. He fed Goblin mornings, and Wendy fed him evenings. The dog was straining at the leash so Jason moved on with him. Tomas and Wendy followed.

"Do you know Aunt Florry?" Wendy asked.

Tomas grinned. "Yes."

"We never knew her before now," Wendy said. "We've never been to New York before, either."

Jason and Goblin turned the corner.

"If we just walk around the block, I guess we can't get lost," Wendy suggested.

"You can't get lost this way," Tomas told her. "The river's right there, behind those piers, so you can't go too far that way. And Greenwich Street's right behind us."

Wendy looked doubtful, but as long as this boy stayed with them, Jason felt they'd be all right.

The three children ranged along the sidewalk, stopping to let Goblin poke his nose into doorways. The street was completely deserted. No cars and no people. Metal awnings covered the sidewalks, so it was like walking along under a porch.

"See these buildings?" Tomas asked. "They're empty! Practically every one—except mine and yours and some of the warehouses and offices."

"How come?" Jason asked.

"Urban renewal."

"What's that?" Wendy demanded.

"It's where they tear down a bunch of old buildings and build something new," Tomas explained. "Everybody likes it except the people who get torn down."

"Are we going to get torn down?" Jason asked, seeing hope for the first time. Maybe they wouldn't have to live there very long.

"Not right away," Tomas said. "They have to tear down these empty ones first."

Sheets of tin covered the storefronts and second-story windows. The children walked around two blocks and came back along Greenwich Street.

"I wonder if supper's ready," Jason said. "I'm hungry."

"Florry spends a long time doing things," Tomas warned them.

"Have you been up there?" Wendy asked him.

"Sure. Sometimes we have coffee. It takes half an hour."

"Have you seen the pigeons?" Jason asked him.

"Sure."

"I don't think she's all there," Wendy stated bluntly.

Tomas made no reply, and Jason felt embarrassed. "Oh, come on, Wen," he said crossly. It wasn't right to talk about your relatives to strangers.

Tomas chuckled. "People around here think she's kind of weird, too. Luke thinks so."

"Who's Luke?" Jason asked.

"He lives on the second floor."

"Below us." Wendy nodded. "Aunt Florry told us. Remember?"

"There he is now!" Tomas pointed. A tall black man was getting out of a car. He crossed the sidewalk to their door. "He's a real good painter. Sometimes he lets me watch."

"You mean he paints pictures?" Wendy asked.

Tomas nodded. "He's so good they let him teach in a college."

Jason and Wendy were silent in the face of this information. They had never known anyone who painted pictures.

Wendy said, "We'd better go up. Maybe she'll hurry faster if she knows we're hungry." She unlocked the door.

They said good-bye, climbed the stairs, turned Goblin into their room, and went on up.

Aunt Florry was fussing from stove to sink. She had cleared off one end of the table by pushing everything to the other end. Three plates were set out.

"Supper's almost ready," she promised. She rinsed a handful of silverware under the tap and gave it to Jason with a towel. "Dry these, please. Everything's so dusty. Just in the time I've been gone."

They sat down to broiled hamburgers, green lima beans, mashed potatoes out of a box, and a lettuce salad. Aunt Florry poured herself a glass of wine and offered some to Jason and Wendy.

Wendy was about to say yes, but Jason said he'd like milk.

"What are you—babies?" Aunt Florry cried with a laugh.

Before either of them could answer, she was saying, "Yes, yes, children *should* drink milk. But I only bought enough for breakfast. Mix a glass of powdered milk!"

Jason said politely that he would drink water. He got up and drew a glass for himself and one for Wendy.

Wendy was feeling annoyed at getting neither wine nor milk. "I don't like lima beans," she said, giving them a disdainful push with her fork.

"Tomorrow night you can cook what you do like," Aunt Florry said cheerfully.

Wendy stared at her and decided she must be joking. "I can't cook," she giggled.

"Can you read?"

"Of course I can read!"

"Then you can read directions," Aunt Florry said. "I have a closetful of canned food. I buy it by the case when there's a bargain. Saves time. All you'll have to do is choose—oh—three things. That should be enough . . . and open the cans and heat them up."

"You mean by myself? Pick the whole meal?"

"Certainly," Aunt Florry said. "I'm far too busy to spend my days cooking for two half-grown children. We'll all take turns. We'll each have a night to cook and a night to wash dishes."

Jason was disconcerted. Did she mean he was going to have to cook, too? He changed the subject, asking politely, "Do you have a job, Aunt Florry?"

"No, no! There's too much to do. I wouldn't have time for a full-time job. It's all I can manage to sit down at my desk a few hours a week as it is." She sighed. "The writing I do seems to take so much research."

"What kind do you do?"

"Well, articles, you know. And some poems and short stories. As soon as I get time, I'm going to write about my pigeons. Don't you think that would be interesting?"

Jason didn't think so, but he nodded. Wendy picked at her lima beans. She was still looking mutinous, but Aunt Florry didn't seem to notice. Her face scrunched up and she began to look angry. "I am very involved with pigeons. You have no idea how the *idiots* in this city go around persecuting them—driving them off buildings when all the poor things want is a place to rest. And making rules against feeding them— It's intolerable! I don't know *what* the country's coming to, when a person isn't allowed to feed the denizens of the air."

"What's a denizen?" Jason asked.

"It's a—well, it's a bird, in this case. Even some members of my bird club are against feeding them! And yet where would their fancy birds be without the humble pigeon to breed from? Oh, I go to their club, and I write their reports for the pigeon breeders' magazine, but my heart's with the little lost ones whose home is the park. I live on the income from my share of the publishing business, you know, but I try to share a little each day with the park pigeons—as well as these upstairs. I don't mean *the* Park," she added, noticing Wendy's questioning look. "I mean the little squares near here."

Jason began to feel concerned for the pigeons, though it was something he had never thought about before. Then he saw Wendy rolling her eyes behind Aunt Florry's back and hanging her tongue out of the corner of her mouth, and he realized he had never heard anyone else get so excited over pigeons. Maybe it *was* a strange thing to do.

However, Aunt Florry went on to talk very reasonably about her collection of canned food, and how she must find clean sheets for their beds. She said she would do that while they did the dishes.

Dessert was canned peaches. Then she showed them the dishpan and dish towel, saying, "In the morning you can fix what you like for breakfast. The toaster's there—" She pointed. "There are eggs in the icebox and dry cereal in the pantry. I'll hunt for your sheets."

She made her way through the furniture, boxes, and piles of papers and opened a door they hadn't had time to notice. It led to a closet that appeared chock-full. Everything was stored in boxes. Aunt Florry began exclaiming that she couldn't find the right box. A moment later she screeched that she had found the cage for Morgan la Fay.

By the time she found the sheets, the dishes were done. Wendy had slopped quite a lot of water on the floor, and Jason suspected she did it on purpose. But Aunt Florry, when she brought the sheets, didn't seem to notice the floor. She had Jason squeeze back through the furniture with her to bring out the cage.

When Wendy saw it, she stopped looking disgruntled and gave a cry of delight. "It's big! Morgan will love it. Can we take it downstairs, now?"

"Right now," Aunt Florry said. "Your sheets, too. It's time you were in bed."

"Where do you sleep, Aunt Florry?" Wendy asked.

Aunt Florry pointed. "There's a room there, like the one you have downstairs."

Wendy said, "We were wondering— Did Daddy ever come visit you?"

"Oh, yes! He and your mother were here once, before you were born. I lived in a tiny apartment then. He thought I should move back to Kansas, but I don't suppose I ever will."

"Why not?"

"I like it better here."

And that's that, Jason thought.

Wendy made a little package of lettuce leaves and leftovers for her rat. They said good night and carried the cage and sheets downstairs.

The big room was dark, but the switch near the door turned on three fluorescent lights of great brilliance.

Elf came mewing, reminding Jason that neither she nor Goblin had been fed. While Wendy introduced Morgan la Fay to her new cage, he went back upstairs to fetch the cans of animal food, bowls, and a can opener.

After he had fed the animals, he sat down on a windowsill and yawned. It was dark outside. "Boy, am I tired," he said.

"Me, too," Wendy agreed. "I think I'll keep Morgan in my room. There's nothing else in there. Will you help me?"

Jason helped carry the cage, and then Wendy called Goblin to come and stay with her, too. "You have Elf," she explained. She plopped down on her mattress, and stared at the black window. "Jason, what's going to become of us?"

"Daddy thought it was okay."

"You know what? I don't think he knew her very well. Even if she was his sister." Her lower lip quivered. "What are we going to *do?*"

"Wait and see, I guess," he said gloomily. "Maybe without Mother and Daddy we'd feel miserable anywhere."

"Maybe."

Reluctantly he said good night and went to his own bed. He was so sad he felt sick. Despite what he had told Wendy, he was sure he felt worse here than he would in some nice place where they had something to look forward to.

He spread the sheets. They got black where they touched the floor. Let them! he thought angrily. If

Aunt Florry was going to make them sleep on the dirty floor, her sheets ought to get dirty.

He found his pajamas in his suitcase, undressed, and went to the light switch.

"Can I turn off the lights?" he called.

"Yes. There's a light in here. Jason—?"

"Yes?"

"Do you still like her?"

"No."

"Me, neither."

Work

WHEN JASON AWOKE NEXT MORNING, HIS HEART sank. The big room looked bare and cheerless. For a moment he thought he was in an empty building. Then he remembered Aunt Florry's crowded apartment, and the dozens of pigeons occupying the top loft. No, the building was far from empty, but anyhow, his stomach felt sick—or empty—he wasn't sure which.

I hope our furniture arrives today, he thought.

Elf was curled beside him like an orange fur doughnut, the only homelike thing in the place. He hugged her and then got up and dressed.

Goblin capered by the door wagging his red, plumed tail and making noises that meant *out!* Jason found the key where Wendy had put it on the windowsill, fastened Goblin on his leash, and led him downstairs.

Outside, he turned to lock the door, hoping Tomas would appear, but he didn't. Jason circled the block with Goblin and went back upstairs.

"Jason?" Wendy called. He heard her moving about in her room. "I took a shower. And then there wasn't any towel. I used my sheet. Ugh!"

She opened her door. She was wearing white shorts and a blue T-shirt. Her brown hair looked damp but combed. "The sheet has to dry."

"Hang it on your clothes tree."

"Good idea!" She flung the sheet over the tree and laughed. "It looks like a ghost with crazy ears."

"This place is grim enough without ghosts."

"It's the windows," Wendy said thoughtfully. "Do you suppose we could wash them?"

"I guess. Let's go eat."

They tiptoed into Aunt Florry's apartment. Quietly they fixed themselves cereal. They felt happier without Aunt Florry.

After breakfast, Wendy found a bottle of something for cleaning windows. She also found a sponge and a rag. They went back to their floor and began to wash the windows. Jason suspected that Wendy felt as he did, that clean windows would somehow annoy Aunt Florry. It was the kind of thing people approved of in Kansas, and the twins were beginning to suspect that Aunt Florry did not think much of Kansas.

By the time she came down to see what they were doing, they had each cleaned three. Jason was doing the last one. Wendy was sweeping.

Aunt Florry came in wearing a sleeveless blue dress like a shift. Jason thought it looked as if she had it on backward. At least, it had flowers embroidered across the back, and none in front.

"You've washed the windows!" she exclaimed. "Well—yes—it does make a difference, doesn't it? How would you like to wash mine? I'll pay you."

That reminded Jason of allowances. He and Wendy had always had their own money, and his father had left plenty—the lawyer said. It was his and Wendy's, as soon as they grew up. But before he could ask about getting some now, Aunt Florry began talking about furniture.

She took them upstairs and showed them a bookcase she thought they should have. In moving things to get it, she came across a square coffee table.

"Take that," she told Wendy, "to put your rat cage on. What about plants—plants for your windows? You can take some of mine, if you'll promise to water them."

Jason frowned, but Wendy said, "I will."

"It'll make the place more cheerful," she whispered to Jason.

"More chairs?" Aunt Florry asked. She unearthed two dusty ones.

Wendy turned up her nose. "They look like they came from an office."

"They did," Aunt Florry said. "I found them on the sidewalk. In perfect condition. Look! Solid oak!" She shook them.

They certainly did look solid, Jason thought.

"Who wants old office chairs—in a house?" Wendy asked.

"Oh, don't be so bourgeois!" Aunt Florry cried. The word was new to Jason. It didn't sound like anything good to be.

"Be bohemian!" Aunt Florry was saying. "Think for yourselves. You've seen too many TV commercials."

"What do you mean?" Jason asked. What was wrong with TV commercials?

"Women scouring sinks, getting their clothes white." She made a face. "There's more to life than that."

"Not if you want to sell soap," Jason said. "TV has to have ads, just like newspapers."

Aunt Florry made an impatient noise. "Here—" she said. "Take these chairs downstairs anyway, and store them if you don't use them. There's too much up here, and you have all kinds of room."

They carried down the chairs, and the table. By the

time they carried down the bookcase, they were hot and tired, and ready for lunch.

"Whew," Jason said when they were by themselves. "I never carried so much furniture in my life. I feel like a mover."

"I feel like a mess," Wendy complained. "Look, my shorts are filthy."

"When's she going to take us someplace?" Jason asked. "There's lots to see in New York."

"When's she going to give us some money?" Wendy asked. "We could go by ourselves if we knew how."

Jason nodded. "I wish she hadn't made us sell our bicycles."

"Jason!" Aunt Florry screeched from the top of the stairs. "Wendy! Lunch!"

They ran upstairs and made their way down the aisle between the furniture.

She waved toward the table. "I've laid out sandwich things. Cheese and lettuce and these nice rolls I bought last night. And mayonnaise. The cheese is a little bit moldy. You can trim off the edges. And there's powdered tea for iced tea." She pointed to a large jar. "I always buy the largest size. It's more economical."

Wendy looked at the cheese in distaste.

"Don't you like cheese?" Aunt Florry asked.

"Not like that. I'll just eat bread and mayonnaise."

"Nonsense!" Aunt Florry cried. "It's like any other cheese, once you trim it a little." She brought a pair of

scissors to the table and snipped neatly around the edge
of the stack. "There. Peel off a slice. Careful! There's
paper in between. Don't eat the paper. Wait a minute." She went to the refrigerator. "Here—here's a
slice of salami to go in the sandwich, too." She dealt
one apiece.

"I'll have just the salami," Wendy said, reaching
for it.

Aunt Florry snatched it back. "Oh, no! No cheese,
no salami."

Indignantly Wendy picked a slice of cheese from
the stack and slapped it on her roll. Aunt Florry gave
her the salami.

Jason watched, fascinated. Aunt Florry squabbled
like another kid. Grown-ups in his experience didn't
act like that. They told you what to do, and you did
it. If you didn't, they ignored you . . . Aunt Florry
acted like a bully. If he and Wendy didn't do what she
told them, she'd probably get even.

The dishes were kept on shelves made from wooden
cheeseboxes of various sizes stacked on top of each
other. Jason got a glass and made himself iced tea.

Wendy ate her sandwich in stony silence.

Aunt Florry finished first and looked from Wendy
to Jason. "Which of you is going to fix supper?"

"Not me," Jason said.

Wendy, her mouth full, gave him a reproachful
look.

"Jason, you put the lunch things away then," Aunt Florry said.

The doorbell rang.

Aunt Florry jumped. "Who can that be? Oh! Maybe it's your furniture!" She rushed off through the room and downstairs.

"I hate her," Wendy said, staring at Jason.

"Aw, she's not that bad." Jason didn't want to get into it just then.

"Yes, she is. She's going to make us do everything. You just watch!" Her eyes filled with tears. "I don't know how to cook supper. This is a pigpen, anyway!"

"Well, you'd better do it. She told you—open three or four cans—"

"Of what?" Wendy sniffed.

"Whatever you like." Jason began to feel exasperated. "Peas, for one, and asparagus . . . and hot tamales . . . Whatever she's got."

"Wait'll you have to do it—" Wendy reminded him. She was mad now and had stopped crying.

Aunt Florry screeched from the stairway— "Children—your furniture is here!"

Wendy jumped up. "Don't forget to put the food away," she reminded Jason nastily, and ran off downstairs.

Jason stood belligerently by the table. He had half a mind to leave everything as it was. But he didn't

quite dare. He didn't know what Aunt Florry would
do, and he felt a little afraid to find out.

He shoved everything into the refrigerator and
washed two glasses, three knives, and the scissors. By
the time he got downstairs Aunt Florry and Wendy
had decided his bed, dresser, and both desks should go
at the end near the potbellied stove.

The moving men set up the beds, and tossed the
twins' own, clean, matching mattresses and box
springs on them. Aunt Florry badgered the men into
carrying the two old mattresses back to her storage
area. She had shipped the twins' bedroom furniture—
rugs, beds, dressers, desks, the rest of their clothing,
and boxes of books. She had convinced them that one
record player was enough. The other had been sold,
together with their bicycles and the other furniture
from their parents' house—except the TV.

Now Aunt Florry said, "We should keep the TV
upstairs. Where we can all watch."

"You could come down here," Wendy said ungra-
ciously. "There's more room."

Aunt Florry showed her teeth. "I may want to
watch it after you go to bed. That would keep Jason
awake."

Before Wendy could think of an answer Aunt
Florry told the moving men: "The TV goes upstairs.
Here—I'll show you. Don't look at the mess! I've been
busy with these children."

"We didn't watch it that much anyhow," Jason said when Aunt Florry had gone.

"We won't have time now," Wendy said bitterly. "We'll be so busy cooking, washing dishes, and walking the dog—forget it!"

The elevator doors opened some minutes later to reveal the two moving men, two trunks containing the twins' winter clothing, and Tomas.

"That's it," one of the men said. "That's all of it."

Goblin trotted over to greet Tomas.

"Nice dog," Tomas said, stepping back.

"He's saying hello," Jason explained.

"Yeah?" Tomas sounded doubtful. He walked about, inspecting Jason's bed, dresser, and the desks with their matching chairs. "This is nice! This came all the way from Kansas?"

Jason nodded. "Wendy's is in here." He showed Tomas his sister's bedroom set, which was painted willoware blue with white figures copied from the china pattern. Her shag rug was blue and white.

Tomas said *wow* again. "My sister should see this."

"It looks silly here," Jason explained. "The windows are supposed to have frilly white curtains and stuff."

"It looks silly anyhow," Wendy said. "I wanted a bunk bed with drawers underneath, like on a ship."

"Last night you were crying because you didn't have curtains," Jason reminded her.

"That was different," Wendy answered.

Tomas touched the white skull. "What's that?"

Wendy told him.

"Ugh!" He went over to watch Morgan la Fay scamper around her cage on the coffee table. "You ought to paint her cage blue, too. Then you'd have a white rat with blue trim."

The twins laughed.

Jason lowered his voice. "Wendy, did you look at Aunt Florry's dress?" he asked. "I think it's on backward."

Tomas nodded. "She always does that. When it gets dirty in front, she turns it around. She doesn't like to waste time doing the laundry. Sometimes I go to the laundromat for her. Now you'll probably have to."

"That, too?" Wendy shrieked. She threw herself back on the bed. Then she sat up. "We might as well be slaves!"

"You'll have to go to Chinatown," Tomas said. "I'll show you."

"Chinatown?" Jason perked up. "Where's that?"

"The other side of Broadway."

"Are there Chinese people there?" Wendy asked.

Tomas began to laugh. "Sure there are Chinese people there."

"There was a Chinese family back home," Jason reminded his sister.

"But not a whole town!"

"It's not really a town," Tomas explained. "It's a part of New York."

"It sounds nice," Wendy said, "but not if we have to do the laundry. What does *she* do?"

Tomas looked puzzled. "She shops a lot," he said at last. "She goes to church sales, and thrift shops—places like that."

"What for?"

He shrugged. "Things—I don't know. Books, sometimes."

Wendy and Jason looked at each other. Aunt Florry had books stacked all round her room, in makeshift boxes, as though she were waiting to buy a bookcase; but she had just given them an empty one. It didn't make sense.

Tomas said, "She spends a lot of time with pigeons. Letting her own out, or feeding the ones outside. She fights a lot with other pigeon feeders."

"What do they fight about?"

"She doesn't want people to feed them bread. She thinks bread isn't good for them. You know that square with trees across from the grocery? If she sees bread there, she borrows the groceryman's broom and sweeps it into the sewer. But she's not so bad, once you get used to her."

Wendy said, "Hah!"

The Statue of Liberty

TOMAS HELPED THE TWINS UNPACK THEIR BOOKS and records, and admired everything. They put a record on the record player, and sat talking while Aunt Florry went off with her shopping cart to buy pigeon feed. When she came back, riding up in the elevator with the 50-pound bag of feed, she stopped at their floor to tell Wendy it was time to start supper. "Be sure to make a salad," she said. "You'll find lettuce and salad dressing in the refrigerator."

"You get to choose what you're going to cook?" Tomas asked.

Wendy nodded and made a face. "I don't know how!"

"It's easy," Tomas said. "Come on, I'll show you."

"You will?" Wendy sounded more hopeful than she had all day.

Tomas started for the door. "Wait till you see. She's got more stuff than the store."

Wendy followed and then looked back at Jason. "You coming?"

"No," he said. "I don't want to learn." He had decided to stick with TV dinners, if he really did have to cook.

But when he found himself alone, he began to feel bored. It would be better when school started. He'd learn how to get around town then, and it would be fun to see the Atlantic Ocean, too. He and Wendy had seen the Pacific, but they'd never been East.

He stood looking out of the window and then decided to look for Aunt Florry.

He found her on the roof, watching the pigeons fly.

"Look at them!" she cried. "Look, look!"

Jason looked. What was so great about a bunch of old pigeons?

"Tomas is showing Wendy how to cook," he told her.

"Good," she said. "Come here, I want to show you something."

He could see a strip of water shining in the sun, and dimly beyond it, more buildings.

"Look," she said. "There's the Statue of Liberty."

It stood on an island in the silvery water, looking like the pictures he'd seen, but smaller.

"Aunt Florry—" He used his most coaxing tone. "Would you take us there?"

"There?" Aunt Florry looked astonished. "What do you want to go there for? You can see it from here."

"But it's not the same. They say you can climb up inside, clear up to her head. Could we, Aunt Florry?"

"I'll think about it," Aunt Florry said. "Let's see how well Wendy makes dinner."

"I'll go tell her," Jason cried and ran across the roof to the door.

Downstairs he found Wendy doing very well. She had cleaned off the whole table and was washing the pink plastic cover. Tomas sat watching.

"What did you do with all the stuff?" Jason asked in astonishment.

"I sorted it out," Wendy said. "I put the books, magazines, and newspapers on that chair, and the empty jars in a sack. I piled the other stuff under the chair. I hope she won't be mad. But it was such a mess."

"If you fix a good dinner we can go to the Statue of Liberty," Jason said. "I just saw it. You can see it from the roof." He turned to Tomas. "Have you been there?"

Tomas said, "I been past it. On the Staten Island ferry."

"You can climb up into it," Jason said. "If she takes us, you want to go?"

"Yeah," Tomas said.

"She practically promised," Jason said. "She said we'd talk about it after she saw how Wendy fixed dinner. What are you fixing, Wen?"

"Mexican," she said smugly. "I thought of it when I found a bag of corn chips. There's chili in that pot, a can of corn and a can of tomatoes together in this pot. Tomas thought of that. You save a pot, see?" She brought a big bowl to the table, took lettuce and cucumber from the refrigerator, and started cutting up the salad. "It's easier than I expected."

Aunt Florry came through the aisle of furniture, talking to herself. She screamed when she saw the table. "Oh! Oh, my! Why did you do it? What did you do with everything? I hope you didn't throw anything away."

"Nothing," Wendy said. "I just stacked things together."

"I told her not to throw anything away," Tomas explained. "A cracker box, that's all."

Aunt Florry took the cracker box out of the garbage bag. "I was saving that for something. What was it? Well, never mind." She stuffed it back into the garbage and turned to the table. "Isn't this nice! Tomas, will you join us? Call Mrs. Malloy and ask if you may."

Tomas went off to the telephone, at the other end of the room.

"Who's Mrs. Malloy?" Wendy asked.

"His foster mother." Aunt Florry looked to see what was cooking. She didn't criticize at all. She merely suggested opening another can of chili; one might not be enough.

Everything tasted all right, and it looked pretty on the table.

"Can we talk about the Statue of Liberty, now?" Jason asked.

Aunt Florry nodded, slyly. "Suppose all three of you help me clean this room tomorrow morning? Then I'll give you the money, and you can go by yourselves."

Jason and Wendy were too surprised to answer. Jason looked about the room. At last he said, "This whole place?"

"I don't see why we have to work, just to get some money," Wendy pouted.

Aunt Florry gave one of her explosive laughs. "Because I want this room cleaned up, and I don't want to do it."

The twins were speechless. They had never heard any grown-up admit such a selfish reason for making them work.

"It's not fair," Jason said. "We have a right to an allowance."

"Do you?" Aunt Florry smiled. Jason didn't like

her smile. He could see too many of her teeth. "What makes you think you have a right?"

He began to feel cold inside. He thought of wicked stepmothers. There were wicked guardians, too. "We always had an allowance," he stated. "And the lawyer said there was plenty of money."

"Ha! I am not your indulgent father," Aunt Florry said. "I expect you to contribute something to this household besides your presence. Tomas earns his allowance."

Jason and Wendy looked at Tomas. Tomas looked at his plate.

"What do you do?" Wendy asked unbelievingly.

Tomas shrugged. "In the summer every day I put out the garbage cans for Mr. Malloy. As soon as they're empty I bring them back in so nobody will steal them. Saturdays I sweep the halls and the stairs. Malloy and me take turns mopping. This week it's his turn."

"That's four flights," Aunt Florry added. "Not just one."

The twins were impressed.

"How much do you get?" Jason asked.

"Five dollars."

Wendy turned up her nose. "We got that much, just for being good."

Tomas chuckled. "I don't get nothing for being good. But I get something for being bad. Not money, either!"

Tomas was bragging. Nevertheless, Jason felt a twinge of envy.

"We don't know how to get to the Statue of Liberty," he said, coming back to the terms of the bargain.

"Tomas knows," Aunt Florry said. "You go straight down the street to the end of the island. There's a boat there."

"I guess we could get there okay," Jason decided. "Do we *have* to clean up this place first?"

"That's the deal," Aunt Florry said.

Jason looked around the room. What did she mean by cleaning it up, anyway? If you dusted every single thing and threw out all the old newspapers and empty jars, it still wouldn't look like any place he'd ever seen anyone living. He and Wendy never should have let her see they could wash windows or sweep. He turned back to the table to see Tomas nodding his head furiously.

"Okay," he said reluctantly. "We'll try. Okay, Wendy?"

"Okay," she agreed.

Aunt Florry gave them each a cupcake for dessert, and then Jason discovered he was expected to wash the dishes.

It's not fair, he thought, because if I get TV dinners, there won't be any dishes for Wendy or Aunt Florry to wash. He slopped through them as fast as he could, while Aunt Florry, Wendy, and Tomas sat and watched television. He had to be somewhat careful, though, because Aunt Florry explained that if you didn't get them clean, the food on them spoiled and you would get very sick. He knew that from school, too, so he was careful.

After the TV program was over, the three children went out to walk Goblin.

"She's mean!" Wendy exclaimed, as soon as they were out on the sidewalk. "And tomorrow's Sunday! We shouldn't have to work on Sunday."

"You get time and a half!" Tomas doubled over with laughter. When he stopped laughing, he said, "I was trying to tell you to say yes! She won't make us work hard. She just never gets around to doing it herself. And besides, you saw yourself, she won't let you throw anything away. How much cleaning can you do in that mess?"

The twins were eating breakfast next morning when Tomas rang the bell. Aunt Florry hadn't come out of her bedroom yet.

"Let's start," Wendy said. "Maybe we can get done before she comes out."

"Where do we start?" Jason asked. Tomas shrugged eloquently.

Wendy studied the room. "You guys could wash the windows, and maybe wash the leaves of that dusty tree. I could sort of sweep the floor. And I could scour the sink. That would be a beginning." No matter what they did, the place was going to look cluttered, but Wendy found that sweeping the kitchen area and Aunt Florry's bathroom made a tremendous improvement. The boys washed windows. They had to move the plants, and all the little tables the plants sat on, in order to get to the windows. Tomas dusted the tables and swept underneath them. Wendy used scouring powder on the sink, then on the stove and refrigerator. Each piece beamed as though it had had its face washed.

Aunt Florry finally came trailing out of her bedroom wearing a long dressing gown, her gray hair standing on end. "What!" she cried. "At it already? I never dreamed you were such hard workers." She looked round the room. "What a difference! I knew you could do it."

Jason stood back and studied the clean windows. Wendy admired her swept floor and white refrigerator. It was hard not to feel pleased with oneself. Jason smiled at Aunt Florry. "We didn't know where else to begin," he said.

"You're doing fine, just fine," she said. "Think how nice it will be, to come back to a clean house."

While Aunt Florry ate breakfast, Wendy put her heart into scouring the bathroom sink and then the toilet. She hadn't realized the toilet was so dirty. She felt like Cinderella, and pretty soon she shed a few tears. How bad her mother must feel if she was looking down from Heaven now. The bathrooms at home were always clean. Perhaps because her mother or the cleaning woman did them. Anyhow, she'd done enough. It wasn't even their bathroom.

When she came out, Aunt Florry and Tomas were drinking coffee. Jason had a cupful, too.

"That takes care of that," she said.

"Well done!" Aunt Florry cried. "Don't the windows look marvelous?" She jumped up from the table. "I'll go look at the bathroom."

A moment later they heard her screech. She rushed out laughing. "Oh! It looks marvelous. The white nearly blinded me! Ha-ha-ha."

"She sounds like the women on TV," Jason said under his breath. "Boorshwa."

Wendy nodded. Still, it was nice to have your work appreciated.

Aunt Florry pointed. "Jason, hand me my purse. You shall each have enough money for a hot dog and a cold drink, the boat and the subway. They close the island at sunset, so I shall expect you back before dark."

She gave them each their share. Tomas went home to change clothes. The twins went downstairs.

Wendy picked a dress from her suitcase that was only slightly wrinkled. It had once been smoothly ironed. She sighed. Ironing, too? Would she have to iron? She couldn't imagine Aunt Florry doing it. She had a hopeful thought: Maybe their clothes were wash and wear.

Tomas was waiting downstairs when they went down, ready.

They crossed the street, and Jason looked back, half expecting to see Aunt Florry watching from one of the clean windows.

"How come she's not worried about us?" he demanded of Wendy in a low voice. "How does she know we won't get lost, or fall off the boat?"

"Maybe she doesn't care," Wendy muttered. "Then she'd never have to give us our money. Come on!" She ran to catch up with Tomas and began asking him where the museum with the dinosaurs was.

From then on, everything was new, especially the subway. Tomas led them down some stairs in the sidewalk. You paid with tokens and went through a turnstile. Lights shone everywhere, like the basement of a building. They found themselves standing on a platform above rows of tracks.

"See that rail over there?" Tomas pointed. "That's the third rail. If you touch that, you're dead."

"How come?" Wendy asked.

"You get electrocuted," Tomas said. "That rail makes the trains run."

The subway train came roaring in and stopped.

Doors slid open. Jason reached for Wendy's hand just as she reached for his. After they were on and seated, he felt silly. There was nothing to it.

The train made almost too much noise to talk, but Tomas yelled above it. "South Ferry! That's the last stop. We get off there." Jason nodded and began to read the ads above the windows. For the first time, he felt he was really in New York.

The ride didn't last long. At South Ferry, they went upstairs with a lot of other people and into a park. Beyond it was the water, and a sign that said LIBERTY ISLAND. They stood in line to buy tickets, but there was no boat, so they bought hot dogs and Cokes while they waited. They felt pleased, being by themselves. All the other kids had people bossing them around, telling them not to do things.

When the boat came, so many people wanted to get on that Tomas and Jason were both afraid it might sink, but a man at the gangplank was counting. When enough got on, the rest had to stay behind.

The boat pulled away from shore and began to cross the harbor. Tomas led them to the rail. "There's the Statue of Liberty!" he shouted.

It looked a lot bigger close up, and to Jason's surprise it was pale green. He had supposed all statues were shiny brown, like Lincoln in the park at home.

"There's the Staten Island ferry!" Tomas pointed

to a flat, orange boat with windows all around. The people around them looked, too.

Tomas nudged Jason and Wendy. "Tourists," he whispered. "They all got cameras."

Jason and Wendy nodded, feeling somehow superior. Then the three of them made a tour of the boat up- and downstairs, and there was nobody to order them to sit down.

"I'm glad Aunt Florry didn't come," Wendy said.

Jason nodded. It was nice to be on their own.

The boat drew up at a wooden landing, and everyone poured onto the island. Another group was waiting in line to go back.

"We better not wait for the last boat," Tomas said, sagely. "We might get home late."

They followed most of the people to the statue, and read Emma Lazarus's poem, which was on a plaque in the wall.

"Give me your . . . huddled masses yearning to breathe free—"

"We had that in school!" Wendy said.

"Me, too," said Tomas.

They stood around waiting to get into the elevator that would take them partway up. When they finally got on, the elevator let them out in a small, smelly space, and they found themselves in line for the spiral staircase. One line was going up, one coming down.

It was hot and took a long, long time. When at last they looked out of the windows in the head, Tomas showed them Brooklyn, Wall Street, Staten Island, and the Verrazano Bridge.

"That's where we came from," he said, pointing to the cluster of tall buildings on lower Manhattan. The scene looked just like pictures of New York. There were ships, too, out by the bridge.

After they came down, they went to look at the souvenirs, and they were thirsty, too. But, all Jason and Wendy had left was their subway fare.

"I've got some money of my own," Tomas said. He bought them each a soda.

"She could have given us some extra," Wendy complained.

"I know what we can do," Tomas said. "If you want to—"

"What?" The twins were ready for any suggestion.

"We can walk home. That way we can spend our subway fare."

"Is it far?" Jason asked.

"Naah. I've walked it." He shrugged. "It ain't close . . . But it ain't too far, either."

They went back to look at the souvenirs. Everything that looked nice was a dollar or more, and everything else was junk.

"I don't care," Wendy finally said. "I'm going to get this tiny little statue."

"What for?" Jason asked.

"I'm going to put it in Morgan la Fay's cage. So she'll know she's an American rat."

Jason whooped. "It's the Statue of *Liberty,* silly. Morgan la Fay's in a cage!"

Wendy was still determined to buy it. "All right, then," she said. "I'll get it for Goblin. He's free. He's as free as we are. He doesn't even have to work."

Jason and Tomas spent their subway fare on another hot dog. They each broke off a third for Wendy, so they all came out even. Then they went and sat on the cement at the edge of the island and dangled their feet over the water. For once, there were no grown-ups to tell them not to fall in.

"This is pretty nice," Jason said. "It was worth doing all that work for."

"Yeah," Tomas said. "Too bad school starts tomorrow."

Jason frowned. "You sure?"

"Sure, I'm sure."

"That's funny," Jason said. "Aunt Florry didn't say anything."

"Maybe she won't let us go," Wendy said. "Maybe she's going to keep us home to work."

They got back to Manhattan in the late afternoon and set out to walk home. It seemed a long way to the twins.

"We always went places in a car or on our bicycles," Wendy complained. "Even to the store."

"New Yorkers walk a lot," Tomas bragged. "Up stairs and down stairs—"

"Who wants to be a New Yorker?" Wendy said crossly.

When they got home, Jason remembered that he had to fix dinner. It was Sunday; the store would be closed. No TV dinners. So Aunt Florry took him to the grocery closet. He picked out a big can of stew, peas (which he liked), and asparagus (which he liked). He chopped off three chunks of lettuce and poured salad dressing on it. And that was that.

Aunt Florry said the combination of vegetables was strange, but she ate it, and Jason had the satisfaction of seeing her wash dishes while he and Wendy watched TV.

After all that walking, they were tired, and Aunt Florry sent them to bed at nine o'clock.

"What about school, Aunt Florry?" Wendy asked.

"School. We'll have to find out about that."

Jason said, "Tomas starts tomorrow."

"Not tomorrow. He must be wrong. I'll call Mrs. Malloy as soon as I get time."

"See," Wendy said when they went downstairs. "She isn't going to let us."

Jason stared at her. "I didn't know you liked school that much."

"I like it better than her! Better than being slaves and prisoners."

"Wendy—you're imagining things again."

"Oh, yeah? You wait." Wendy closed her bedroom door, leaving Jason alone in the big room, which still looked bare, despite the furniture. Elf was sleeping on the bed, so once there, himself, he held the cat in his arms and coaxed Goblin to climb in, too.

Aunt Florry wasn't cruel. But she was sure strange!

More Work

MONDAY MORNING AUNT FLORRY TOLD JASON THAT he could have five dollars a week if he would feed the pigeons every morning and give them clean water. Wendy could have five dollars if she would take the laundry to Chinatown once a week, put it in the coin machines, then bring it home and hang it on the roof to dry.

"Instead of cooking?" Jason asked.

"No, no! Cooking remains the same. We still take turns with the cooking. My job will be to do the shopping—including bringing home food for your pets."

"I guess you spend a lot of time writing," Wendy said.

"Er—yes. That's right. I often spend the whole day at the library."

The twins didn't seem to have much choice but to agree. Reluctantly Jason said, "Okay."

"All right," Aunt Florry said, "Wendy you wash the dishes like a good girl while I take Jason up and show him what has to be done for our fine, feathered friends. Don't you come. Two strange people will scare them."

"I don't want to come," Wendy said.

Aunt Florry replied absentmindedly, "Good," and led the way into the hall and up the stairs.

The top floor was airless and hot, and smelled of pigeons and pigeon feed. Jason decided Wendy had the best deal. Her job would take longer, but it was only once a week.

As soon as Aunt Florry took him through the wire gate, pigeons came flying and landed on them both. Jason wanted to knock them away from his head, but when he flailed out, Aunt Florry screamed, "No, no! They won't hurt you."

Stupid pigeons, Jason thought. Wait'll she's not here. I'll teach them to land on me!

First he had to fill two pans with water so the birds could bathe. Next Aunt Florry had him fill a 2-pound coffee can with feed and pour it into the feeder. She also showed him how to wash their drinking pan, which sat in the sink. The pan was covered with wire screen so the birds couldn't bathe there.

By the time that was done, Aunt Florry said the

birds had had enough bathing. So he had to pick up the pans and empty them.

"Are they good to eat?" he asked tentatively. He didn't relish the idea.

"Don't say that!" Aunt Florry cried over the noise of running water. "They're pets! Aren't you, my fine, feathered pidgies?" she cooed to the row of watching red eyes.

He didn't understand. What fun could you have with a pigeon? He guessed Aunt Florry liked to watch them fly, but they didn't fly like free birds. They flew round and round, as if they had a string attached.

"There—that's not hard, is it?" she asked when they were letting themselves out of the pen. "Don't ever forget to hook this door," she cautioned, not giving him a chance to say whether feeding pigeons was too hard or not.

She spent the rest of the morning rounding up dirty clothes.

"I'll need a truck!" Wendy grumbled.

There was cheese again for lunch. Aunt Florry thought Morgan la Fay should eat the moldy parts, but Wendy took a good piece for Morgan, when Aunt Florry wasn't looking.

After lunch, Aunt Florry sorted the wash into bags and stuffed them into the shopping cart. It wasn't too bad, once it all got together, Wendy admitted.

Jason decided to go, too. He wanted to see Chinatown. Aunt Florry went downstairs with them and pointed them in the right direction.

"Go along this street until you come to a little park. You'll see Chinese people sitting in the park, and you'll know you're in Chinatown. Then ask where the laundromat is."

They took Goblin for company and were glad they had. They felt as if they were going to walk forever. And every way they looked they saw tall buildings.

"I wonder how you get to the country," Wendy said.

"I guess you don't," Jason said.

They knew when they finally reached Chinatown because the sidewalks became crowded with people—Chinese-looking people. The streets seemed narrower. Tiny stores showed windows filled with strange wares. Small Chinese children were playing in the park.

"Look, even the telephone booth is Chinese!" Jason pointed to one, its familiar shape embellished with an oriental temple roof of red and gold.

"And the streetlights!" Wendy exclaimed. They, too, had pagoda shapes.

They had to ask several times, but eventually they found their way to the laundromat, which was small and crowded. The Chinese woman who was the proprietor showed Wendy how to use the machines. And once she had put in the clothes, the soap, and the money, there was nothing more to do.

"I wonder if we could wait in the park," Wendy said.

"Ask her," Jason suggested.

The Chinese woman nodded. "You come back," she said.

They looked into store windows and then went to the park, which was nothing but trees, hard-packed earth, and benches. Across the street a store offered pizza through a window on the sidewalk.

"I wish we had some money," Jason said. "When do you suppose she'll give us our five dollars? At the end of the week?"

"I've got some," Wendy said.

"You have?"

Wendy nodded. "I took some out of my bank. Come on, I'll buy two slices."

While they were waiting for the pizza, Jason asked, "How much money do you have? Do you mind telling?"

"Forty-eight dollars."

Jason whistled.

"You?" she asked.

He made a face. "Thirty, maybe. Listen, you better not spend any more. We might need it."

"What for?"

"We might want to run away."

Wendy's blue eyes widened. "Where?"

Jason thrust out his lower lip. "There's Mother's uncle in western Kansas. I don't know if you remember, but he sent a telegram. He couldn't come to the funeral because they were harvesting."

Wendy said thoughtfully, "I remember. It'd be more fun to work on a farm than here."

"We don't know if he'd want us," Jason said. "But we can keep it in mind."

Their slices of pizza came, and Jason's spirits rose. They had money, and they had someplace to go, if worst came to worst.

They ate the pizza, gave the crusts to Goblin, and went back to the laundromat. Jason helped Wendy dump the wet laundry into the bags and they started back to Aunt Florry's. Wendy fussed and groaned over pulling the cart, heavier now that the clothes were wet, but Jason said she might as well get used to it.

When they were nearly home, someone called their names. They turned, and Tomas came running up, carrying two spiral notebooks. He was wearing shoes instead of rubber sandals, and a new shirt and pants.

"You didn't come to school!" he shouted.

"Was it today?" Wendy cried.

"Sure it was." Tomas nodded. "I told you it was."

"Aunt Florry said it wasn't," Jason told him. "She said she'd call your mother—"

"Not my mother," Tomas interrupted. "My foster mother. Like a godmother."

"Well, whoever," Jason said. "Aunt Florry said she'd ask her."

"You been to the laundromat?" Tomas asked.

"We've been learning our jobs," Wendy explained. "Jason learned how to feed pigeons—"

"And how to bathe them," Jason added.

"And I learned how to do the washing," Wendy went on. "That's what we have to do for an allowance. Tomorrow she'll probably think up more."

"You better go to school," Tomas said. "She has to let you go to school."

"Where is it?" Jason asked.

"You take the bus to 17th Street. It's right down the block."

"We don't have any money," Wendy reminded him. "Unless we spend our savings."

Jason said, "Ask for your money, Wendy. You've done your work. You can lend me some till I get mine."

"You don't have to have money—once you're going," Tomas told them. "You get a bus pass."

"You do?" Jason's eyes opened wider.

"Sure," Tomas said. "And free lunches."

"That's a good reason for going," Wendy said. "I'm tired of moldy cheese."

"She was always trying to give cheese to Mrs. Malloy," Tomas said. "Mr. Malloy finally told her we didn't want anymore."

"Where does she get it?" Wendy wondered.

"Around the corner," Tomas said. "A company throws it out. If it gets moldy in the supermarkets, they have to take it back. It's good-enough cheese—"

"But every day?" Jason asked, and made them all laugh.

"What if she won't let us go?" Wendy asked.

"She has to let you go," Tomas said. "It's the law."

Jason said, "Yeah, but the law doesn't know we're here."

"Sneak out tomorrow and go with me. Once you get registered, if you don't go, the truancy will come looking for you."

"Marvelous," said Wendy. "Then they'll be after her, and we can say she made us stay out!"

"Right," Tomas said.

"Come on," Wendy said. "Let's get this laundry hung up. Then I'll ask for the money."

Tomas knew how to work the elevator, but they had to carry the cart up the last flight to the roof.

Aunt Florry was there, watching the pigeons fly. "How nice!" she cried. "Look at all those clean clothes."

The clothespins were at the top of the stairs. Tomas

wiped the soot off the rope lines with a dry rag, then he and Jason sat and talked to Aunt Florry, while Wendy worked.

Wendy began to feel put upon, hanging up the clothes. Look at them, sitting around, while she worked her fingers to the bone. Aunt Florry had better give her five dollars, she thought, or she'd tell a policeman! Furthermore, she didn't think she'd lend Jason any. He could stay home with Aunt Florry if he liked her so much. She'd go to school by herself . . . if Tomas would show her the way.

At last, however, the clothes were all hung up, and she felt a little better. Everyone was ready to go in, including the pigeons.

"Aunt Florry has to cook supper tonight," Jason reminded Wendy when the three of them were alone on the third floor.

"You forgot to ask for the money," Tomas said.

"I'll do it now." Wendy jumped up.

"She's pretty brave," Tomas said when she had left the room. "I'd be scared to ask Florry for money."

"It's our money," Jason said indignantly. "Our father left it to us."

"She likes to keep things," Tomas muttered.

But this time she didn't. Wendy came back, waving a five-dollar bill.

"What time is school?" she asked Tomas.

"Eight-forty," he said. "Maybe you ought to go

early. So you can register and stuff. Do you have records from your old school?"

Wendy gasped. "We have records, but we don't have a clock!"

They all three sat still a moment. "*I* know!" Tomas said. "Ask Luke Harrison to call you. He goes to school! He goes clear to Brooklyn."

"Won't he think it's funny?"

"Naaah!" Tomas said. "He knows how she is. Come on, let's ask now. I have to be getting home."

The twins followed him down one flight. He knocked on a door that matched theirs.

A deep voice called, "Yeah!" Footsteps came across a bare floor, and Luke Harrison opened the door.

"Hi," Tomas said.

Luke Harrison had a paintbrush in one hand, like painters in the movies. His blue jeans were streaked with paint.

"Come in." He looked somberly at Jason and Wendy. They followed Tomas into a room like their own. Big paintings hung on the walls. An easel with another painting stood in one corner. The pictures were of black people with fires, lightning, and things blazing. One looked like Martin Luther King.

"I take it you're Florry's kin," Luke said.

"I'm Jason," Jason said. "This is my sister Wendy."

Luke shook Jason's hand. "I was sorry to hear about your parents," he said.

Jason and Wendy nodded and looked at the floor. It was hard to be reminded.

"They want to ask a favor," Tomas said. He explained how they wanted to sneak off to school.

Luke threw back his head and laughed. "That don't say much for Florry, does it? If school's better."

Jason grinned politely. Grown-ups always expected kids to hate school. But it was okay, if the teachers were good.

Luke said he'd knock on their door at seven.

"We'd better go," Wendy said, looking over her shoulder. "Aunt Florry's cooking dinner."

Luke went back to painting, and they said good-bye.

Jason went downstairs with Tomas to lock the door after him, and Wendy went upstairs to choose something to wear the next day.

"Tomas says you can wear anything," Jason said when he found her staring into her closet. "Even shorts. But you can't go barefoot."

Wendy turned with a laugh. "Won't she be surprised?"

Jason laughed, too. "We'll leave her a note."

Jason had to do the dishes after supper, and Wendy had to bring down the dry clothes in a basket. It took four trips. She piled them in Aunt Florry's bedroom on top of a long desk already heaped with books and paper.

Then, before they went to bed, they took Goblin out.

"I have to feed those pigeons in the morning," Jason said. "Will you walk Goblin?"

"Sure," Wendy said. "I hope she doesn't wake up while we're getting breakfast."

"She never does."

"No, but tomorrow she might."

They had never looked forward to school so much.

Rescuing Things

"WHAT'S THE NAME OF THE SCHOOL?" JASON ASKED Tomas while they waited for the city bus.

"I.S. Seventy," Tomas said.

"I.S. Seventy?" Wendy echoed. "What kind of a name is that?"

"It's not a name, it's a number," Tomas said. "I.S. means Intermediate School."

The bus came, so there was no time for the twins to express their feelings about a school with a name like that. The bus driver knew Tomas, and when Tomas told him the twins were going to I.S. 70, he let them ride free.

After school, Jason found Tomas waiting outside. Wendy came soon after.

"Did you get your bus pass?" Tomas asked.

The twins flashed them in front of him.

"Okay. Now I'll show you how to get home." He set off in a new direction.

"This isn't the way we came," Jason said.

"That's the *uptown* bus," Tomas said briskly. "Now we gotta take the *downtown* bus."

They sat in the bus, holding their books and watching buildings flash by. Jason noticed that Wendy was very quiet, but he understood. He didn't feel much like talking, himself, though there was a lot to talk about. Their classes were separate. They had seen each other only at lunchtime.

At last when they were walking home from the bus, Wendy said, "I don't like it much. I wouldn't mind if she kept us home."

Jason nodded. "It's sure different."

"How?" Tomas asked. "School is school."

Jason shook his head. He couldn't explain. Not now when I.S. 70 was so new. He needed to talk to Wendy first.

"I hope she won't be mad," Jason said, dragging his feet.

"Me, too," Wendy said.

"How can she be?" Tomas asked. "You got a right to go to school."

Nevertheless, when he left them to go into his own doorway, they felt apprehensive.

They moved on, Jason unlocked their door, and they started upstairs.

"We *had* to go," Wendy said stoutly.

Quietly, they let themselves into their loft and put their books on their desks. Goblin danced and wagged. Elf jumped down from the windowsill, yawning and stretching.

"Let's go," Wendy said, pushing her hair back.

They had always been able to sense each other's moods. Now their mood was the same, and they acted the same. They bounded up the stairs to Aunt Florry's with a great show of bravado.

"We're home!" Wendy called, opening the door. "Aunt Florry?"

Aunt Florry came out of her bedroom looking hot and dusty. "So much to put away!" she exclaimed. Behind her Jason glimpsed the pile of clean laundry still sitting where Wendy had laid it. "So Tomas took you to school! I thought you were in your room until after I called Mrs. Malloy. Then I found your note."

Jason flashed a look at Wendy, who gave a little laugh.

"We didn't think you'd mind," she said. "We didn't want to wake you."

"No, no! Of course I don't mind. Do what you want! You fed the pigeons, didn't you, Jason?"

"Yes, Aunt Florry."

"Well, well. Tell me about school. Would you like to share a soda?"

The twins looked at each other. It was silly, but they couldn't help feeling they had misbehaved and were escaping punishment. Under the circumstances, they thought it was better not to fuss about splitting one soda. They sat around the table, which was the only space to sit, drinking.

"Well, how was it?" Aunt Florry asked brightly.

Wendy wrinkled her nose. Jason could think of nothing to say.

"The kids are all pretty different," Wendy said at last. "They yell a lot."

"Yeah," Jason agreed. "And there's a girl in my class named Tenderleaf."

"Tenderleaf!" Aunt Florry exclaimed.

"Yep. Tenderleaf Ruiz, or something like that."

"That *is* different!"

Wendy giggled. "We got bus passes," she said then, "and our books. And for lunch we had hot dogs and milk."

"But we have to buy notebook paper," Jason said. "Aunt Florry, could I have my allowance now?"

"We have a lot of studying," Wendy said, to reinforce his request. "Themes and stuff."

Grudgingly, it seemed, Aunt Florry went to her purse. She gave Jason a ten-dollar bill and told him to get it changed at the office-supply store by the bus stop.

"Whew!" Jason said when they were walking down the street with Goblin. "I'm glad she wasn't mad."

"I didn't really think she would be," Wendy said.

"Then why were you scared?"

"I wasn't scared—exactly."

"You were, too!"

"Well, anyway," Wendy said, "you know what I think? I think she's glad we're out of her way. I think she doesn't want us to know what she does all day."

"Why?"

"I don't know. I just think that."

Jason thought Wendy was being too imaginative again.

They bought the notebook paper they needed, then went home and did homework. Before Wendy finished, she had to stop and get supper.

Alone, Jason stared absentmindedly into the shadowy corner by the bathroom where they had stored the office chairs Aunt Florry had made them take. Something that looked like a small table had been put there, too. He stood up and went over to look at it. Sure enough, it was a small, dusty table. Behind it was a large picture frame. He wondered where they had come from. The table looked as if it had been stored in somebody's attic for a hundred years.

That night when Jason went out to walk Goblin, Tomas joined him.

"Malloy says they've started tearing down," Tomas announced. "Let's go look."

"Wow!" he cried when they rounded the corner into the street behind theirs. "They built a sidewalk bridge already!"

Sure enough, the metal awnings in front of the two corner buildings had been taken down. In their place, there was a sturdy wooden platform roof over the sidewalk, so passersby would not be hit by falling bricks.

"A sidewalk bridge . . ." Jason liked learning the names of things—everything. Someday he was going to be a newspaperman and would need to know about everything. His father had known as much as the encyclopedia—or almost. Jason's throat felt twisted. If only his father had known about the storm . . . they wouldn't have been flying in that small plane.

"Then they'll tear down the next two, and the next, and pretty soon there'll be nothing left," Tomas was saying.

"Then we can play ball here," Jason said. He hadn't seen one space big enough to play baseball.

"Are you kidding?" Tomas waved his arms. "They'll build something else *up*. We won't be here, anyway; we'll be torn down, too."

"Where'll we be?"

"I'll be in the project," Tomas said. "I don't know where you'll be."

"Does my aunt know—that it's being torn down?"

"Sure she knows. She got a 'viction notice same as we did."

"Aunt Florry—" he asked at supper the next evening. He had bought TV dinners, and everyone had just finished their favorite kind. Aunt Florry was going to wash the trays and save them.

"Aunt Florry, where are we going to move when they tear down this building?"

"Shh!" she cried. "Don't say that! They're not going to tear down this building for a long, long time."

"They've started on the ones over there."

"That doesn't mean anything. They're empty."

"But when they do—"

"Don't cross your bridges till you come to them," she advised.

That night he dreamed the sidewalk bridge had come to them. He saw Aunt Florry crossing it and climbing down a ladder. Behind her was Wendy with Morgan la Fay, then came Goblin, and he came last with Elf. Goblin had trouble getting down the ladder, but a big fireman helped. . . .

School settled down and became pretty much like school in Kansas, except that the kids didn't go to each other's houses afterward. At least they didn't seem to. Tomas always came home.

Cooking wasn't too bad, especially when someone else was going to wash the dishes. Wendy even made a pizza once from a mix, and then Jason began making chocolate tapioca pudding from a box, because he loved it and nobody else would make it. One thing about Aunt Florry, she never criticized the meals they fixed. Jason made tapioca pudding for dessert every time his turn came for two weeks and nobody complained.

He didn't mind feeding and watering the pigeons; sometimes Wendy did it for him, when it got too monotonous. And he generally went with her to do the washing. Even the bare space they called home was beginning to seem less strange. Maybe because it was filling up with furniture.

The day after he discovered the table and picture frame stored in their room, Jason noticed that Aunt Florry had added two chairs without seats and a small wooden cabinet with a mirror.

When Wendy came downstairs from ironing, he showed her the growing collection.

"Where does she get them?" he wondered.

"Tomas said she goes to sales and thrift shops. Maybe she gets them there. You know what I think?"

"What?"

"I think she never does any work—I mean, real,

grown-up people's work. I think she does just what she likes."

"Like collecting old furniture?"

"Yes, and pigeons, and going to the library, and watching animal programs on TV. And she's always talking about something free she went to."

The next day a beat-up dresser and a small blue bookcase joined the group.

They didn't ask Aunt Florry about the furniture. Instead, they pretended not to notice. And every day there was more, until it lined the wall between their bathroom and the closet.

"We never use that side of the room," Jason said, "but what if she doesn't stop?"

"Right!" Wendy agreed. "What if she squeezes us into a corner, like upstairs? Besides, it's gloomy." Her eyes began to dance. "She didn't ask us if she could move it in. Let's move it out!"

"Where? You mean throw it out?"

"No! I mean move it. Hide it here and there. Or use it. Like this small table. We could use that in the bathroom." She dusted it and bore it off.

Coming back to find Jason still in contemplation, she said, "We can't get rid of everything, but if we clear out some, she may get the message and stop putting it here."

"She may," he admitted. "On the other hand, she

may figure she has room for that much more. But we could put that wooden cabinet over the sink," he added hastily before Wendy could call him a spoil-sport.

The cabinet had metal eyes to hang from, so he got a hammer, climbed on a chair, and drove two big nails into the wooden partition above the sink, being careful to space the nails the right distance apart to fit the eyes. When he tried to lift the cabinet up to the nails, he found it heavy and awkward, but with Wendy's help he managed.

Wendy took the little blue bookcase into her room. Aunt Florry was out somewhere—feeding pigeons, probably—so they carried the chairs without seats up to the pigeon loft and stored them with the things there. They put a stool up there, too, and then took a small metal table, like an old typewriter table, into Aunt Florry's domain, and put it under her tall telephone table.

While they were still on Aunt Florry's floor, they heard someone coming upstairs, but it was only Luke coming home. They ran down and asked him if he needed a dresser. He said it might be useful and helped move it down. By the time that was done, the twins were dirty and tired.

"That's enough," Jason said, laughing. "Let's wait and see if she notices. Meantime, we can figure out more hiding places."

But, Aunt Florry, when she came home, was in no mood to notice furniture. She was very excited, carrying a paper.

"Listen, children! Listen to this!" she called, coming into their room. "The *Times* has printed my letter! Listen!" And she read the letter:

Dear Editor:

Have those people who hate pigeons ever thought what our city would be like without them? No swoop and flutter of wings to soften the hard outlines of glass and concrete. No soft cooing in the springtime, no friendly company in the park. What a bare city it would be!

My message, however, is not to pigeon haters, but to pigeon lovers. Are you aware of the harm done to them by white bread—eggs unhatched, adults devitalized? Nature designed pigeons to eat grain. Pigeon feeders, give a thought to nutrition! Spend a few pennies for good, wholesome corn, millet, barley or dried peas.

A True Pigeon Lover

She looked triumphantly at the twins. "What do you think of that?"

"Nice, Aunt Florry!" Wendy peered over her aunt's arm. "They should've put your name."

"No, no," Aunt Florry said, withdrawing almost

shyly. "I'm not looking for publicity." She frowned. "My letter was much longer, but I guess they got the sense of it."

"*Is* bread bad for them?" Jason asked.

"Of course it is! Isn't that what I'm saying?"

"Yes, but how do you know?"

"It stands to reason!" she stated, making for the door. "I must go call our club president. Obviously the *Times* agrees with me. I'm going to have copies made and hand them out."

"I still don't see how she knows bread's bad for them," Jason insisted.

"Who cares? She didn't see the furniture was gone, that's what's important."

As a matter of fact, as time went on, Aunt Florry never seemed to miss any furniture, nor did she notice pieces turning up in new places. The twins tucked things here and there until they had reduced the amount stored in their loft by about one-third, in spite of the fact that now and then a new piece arrived.

Then Aunt Florry started bringing in stones.

One night at supper she said, "Oh! They're tearing down that brick building with the terra-cotta bas-relief."

The twins looked blank.

"Look at it when you go out with Goblin," she

directed. "The brick building on the corner. Look at the beautiful decoration over the windows and at the corners. Oh! It's a shame—a shame—to destroy that. I telephoned the Brooklyn Museum, but I couldn't get anyone interested. It should be saved. Be sure to look at it."

That evening when Jason started out with Goblin, Wendy said, "I'm coming, too. I want to see what she means."

They had never really looked at the buildings around them before. But, now they stood across the street from the one Aunt Florry had mentioned and craned their necks.

"I guess that's what she means," Wendy said, "those curly parts above the doorway and up there at the top."

"They are pretty," Jason conceded. He looked up and down the street. "None of the other buildings have them."

When they got home from school next day, they found Aunt Florry directing a man with a hand truck into the elevator. On the hand truck were two big chunks of carved, red stone. Each chunk was the size of a portable TV, but a lot heavier.

"Look! Look!" Aunt Florry cried when she saw the

twins. "Look what I've rescued. They just hurled them down, though I screamed at them to be careful. There are more! I'm going to try to save the best ones."

Each carving was a looped garland of fruit and leaves. The edges were jagged, but the carvings looked okay.

"You know, of course," she said, riding up in the elevator, "that that's bas-relief, when the sculpture sticks out only a little way."

"What's the other word you said—terra-cotta?" Jason asked.

"Terra-cotta? Ah, that's Italian for cooked earth. That's what it is—baked clay. They mold it into building blocks and then bake it. You'll see it on lots of buildings in New York, but this one is particularly ornate. It was built in—oh, I'd say 1880."

The trouble with Aunt Florry, Jason thought, was that she always told you more than you wanted to know.

"Aren't they lovely?" She seemed to want the twins to admire them.

"I guess so," Jason said dutifully. It felt like he was admiring a brick.

"Where are you going to put them?" Wendy ventured to ask. Jason had also been wondering.

"In the hall, I thought. Just till I find someone who wants them."

Jason thought that might be a long time.

"They'd look lovely in a garden," Aunt Florry said. "With ivy."

The twins nodded politely.

"There are more!" Aunt Florry exclaimed. "And we've got to rescue them! We have to get them tonight because tomorrow they'll throw down more bricks."

The twins put their books in their room and obediently tagged along. They were reluctant, and yet half curious. The man with the hand truck had been hired by Aunt Florry, and if he thought it was strange to save broken blocks of masonry, he didn't say so.

He stood by while Aunt Florry clambered over the rubble, hunting for more carved pieces. People who passed stared at her, of course, and that made Jason feel silly. He tried to look as if he wasn't with her by gazing in the other direction. But in a minute she was screeching, "Jason! Wendy! Look! Here are two small ones you can carry. Come up here! I'll hand them to you."

Wendy rolled her eyes at Jason before climbing the brick pile. Aunt Florry shrieked at her to be careful.

The pieces they had to carry were about as heavy as three bricks together. Aunt Florry called them dentils. They were really for decoration, but they appeared to hold up the eaves. Jason thought of *dentals*—that's what they looked like—a row of teeth—when he saw the ones in place over the building across the street.

"She *is* crazy," Jason said, as soon as they got around the corner with their burdens. "Everybody was looking at her."

"At least she's not putting them in our room," Wendy commented.

Aunt Florry worked and worked. She wouldn't give up until she had turned over practically the whole top layer of bricks and found about ten big chunks. And the twins carried more than one load home.

"Imagine doing this back in Kansas," Jason said. "Everybody'd stop and ask what you were doing."

"And then they'd lock you up," Wendy panted. The carving she was carrying weighed about twice as much as the suitcase she'd fussed about, Jason noticed, but now she wasn't saying a word about the weight. There was too much else to think about.

Aunt Florry lined their whole hallway with terracotta carvings. For a few days the twins cracked their ankles on jutting corners, but then they got used to walking next to the other wall and became quite fond of the designs.

The following week Jason discovered where the furniture came from.

He and Tomas were walking Goblin. It was dark, almost bedtime. They were rounding a corner when

Tomas jumped back and flattened himself against the building, his finger to his lips. Jason moved back, pulling Goblin to him.

"Florry!" Tomas whispered, his dark eyes sparkling. "Look!" He beckoned Jason up close.

Together they peered round the corner. She had stopped in front of a door that someone had broken open. She glanced up and down the empty street and then slipped inside. The light from her flashlight gleamed through a crack.

Jason and Tomas looked at each other round-eyed.

"What's she doing?" Jason asked. Since Tomas didn't know either, they decided to wait and spy on her.

Jason walked Goblin up and down the side street while Tomas kept watch. At last he beckoned wildly.

Peeking round the corner, Jason saw Aunt Florry put a rocking chair on the sidewalk. It had one rocker and no seat. She disappeared into the building again and this time brought out a box full of something. They watched while she carried the rocking chair to the far corner, nearer home. She set it down and went back for the box. In relays she carried both things out of sight.

Jason smote his forehead. *"That's* where she gets that junk! Have you seen our place? She's filling it up!"

"Wendy showed me the carvings," Tomas said.

"No, in our room. Whose stuff is it? That's what I'd like to know."

Tomas shrugged. "Nobody's. The people went off and left it."

"Have you been in any of them?" Jason asked, indicating the buildings. He had never thought before of what might be inside of them.

Tomas dug his hands in his pockets and shivered. "Not me! Your aunt's not scared of nothing."

"We could go in some afternoon," Jason suggested.

Tomas shook his head. "I looked in some doors. It's dark inside! The windows are tinned over. You might fall down an elevator."

Jason rushed home to tell Wendy, not wholly convinced he didn't want to visit the empty buildings. In fact, it all sounded a bit daring and attractive. He didn't meet Aunt Florry. She had probably used the elevator. But the next afternoon the rocker appeared in their room.

"I'm going to ask her to take me," Jason said.

"Me, too!" said Wendy.

The Old Hotel

THAT EVENING AT THE SUPPER TABLE JASON SAID, "Aunt Florry, we saw you coming out of an empty building last night."

For a moment Aunt Florry looked as though she would deny it. Then she said cautiously, "Yes, I found some perfectly good furniture."

"Could we go with you next time?" Wendy coaxed.

Aunt Florry hooted. "I didn't suppose you'd do anything so adventurous!" But she added quickly, "Of course, you can come if you want to. You can help carry things."

On Saturday morning, Jason walked to Chinatown with Wendy to do the laundry. When they got back, Aunt Florry had lunch ready.

"Would you like to explore a building today?" she asked while they were eating.

Jason said, "Sure!"

Wendy made a muffled sound around a mouthful of bread and cheese and nodded her head.

"You must promise to be very quiet and follow me, then. I have only one flashlight."

After lunch, Aunt Florry told them to get the shopping cart, while she got her bag of tools. They went downstairs together, and while Aunt Florry locked the door, Jason looked toward Tomas's building. He didn't see Tomas, and decided that was all right. Aunt Florry might object to taking three kids. Besides, Tomas hadn't seemed very eager about it the night they'd seen Aunt Florry.

The day had turned cold and gloomy. "More like November than October," Aunt Florry said.

They went around the corner and through the deserted streets. It reminded Jason of a ghost town.

"We're going into an old hotel," Aunt Florry told them. "It's been closed for years, and we must be careful going in. If the police see us, they might accuse us of breaking the padlock. I'd never break in. The bums do that, to get the lead and copper out of the old toilets."

"What for?" Jason asked.

"To sell, naturally."

"Is it all right to go in?" Wendy asked. "I mean, what if we got put in jail?"

"No, no! Nobody will bother us," Aunt Florry

said. "The police don't care, as long as we're not breaking in. All the same, what they don't know won't hurt them. The former tenants were supposed to leave the buildings broom clean. So officially they're empty."

They came to the door Aunt Florry had in mind. She looked up and down the street, and then told them to scoot inside. She followed, with the shopping cart.

Jason felt his way through a pair of tall inner doors and found himself on a wide staircase. Wendy was right behind him. He had become used to dark stairs, so he found there was enough light to see by. The two went up on tiptoe. The air felt damper and colder inside than outside. The bannister felt damp and gritty. Chunks of plaster crunched underfoot. At the top they reached an open room and then stopped to look around. The woodwork had been painted dark brown. The walls were brown halfway up, then mustard yellow.

Jason felt tense and excited. The noise from the street sounded muffled because of the tin covering the windows. But there were enough places where the tin had pulled away that patches of daylight shone through into the rooms and the two halls, which ran to the right and left.

Wendy gave him a grin, and he giggled. Aunt Florry shushed him sternly and led them down the front hall.

At first they followed her from room to empty room, but then Wendy darted into a room on her own. In a loud whisper Aunt Florry told her to wait.

Wendy reappeared in the doorway. "Here's a dresser!"

Aunt Florry whisked into the room on Wendy's heels. Jason crowded in, too. The small room held a bare iron bedstead and a dresser, painted brown. Aunt Florry suppressed a shriek.

"Oak! Oak, under all that paint! Oh! Marvelous!"

Many of the remaining rooms had dressers, too. Some had washstands as well. Aunt Florry went into ecstasies. "Oh!" she kept exclaiming. "We must rescue them! Everyone wants oak!"

Not all the furniture was rescuable, to Jason's relief. On some, drawers were missing. Several pieces, owing to the dampness, had come unglued.

When their inventory of the front hall was complete, they explored the back hall, which rambled around in the shape of an *L*. One back room had been some sort of kitchen, with all kinds of things piled into it. Aunt Florry stopped to paw through the accumulation. The twins, escaping, crept up to the top floor by the back stairs. The windows there were not tinned over. The doors were open, and the halls were full of light, drier, and warmer.

At first they walked very quietly and did not speak at all. They looked into room after room and found them empty except for bedsteads, springs and more dressers. As they got used to the place, they became bolder.

"Isn't it grim?" Wendy said in a low voice. "How would you like to live *here?*"

"Maybe the people who came didn't stay long," Jason said hopefully. "Just overnight."

They were approaching the wide, main staircase when Wendy stiffened. Jason bumped into her.

"Someone's coming!" she whispered.

Jason heard ascending footsteps—heavy footsteps. The twins stood alert, ready to run, but standing their ground till they saw who it was. If it was a policeman, they shouldn't run, of course.

It was not a policeman. They saw a dark, uncovered head first, then a tweed jacket. A man dressed like that had no more right to be here than they had.

Jason shuffled his feet to announce their presence.

"Hello!" the man exclaimed, catching sight of them. "Quite a place here." His eyes twinkled and his voice sounded friendly.

"Yes," Jason agreed. "We're exploring it with our aunt."

"Oh?" the man said. "Have you found anything good?"

"Some old dressers," Jason said. "She thinks they're good."

"So they are," the man said, "if you like to strip paint. I'm here to get one myself. I'm just taking a look around first." He went off down the hall, peering into rooms.

"We better go downstairs," Jason said. It was funny, but the place had suddenly become very ordinary. Like making your way around a museum. You expected to meet people.

They found Aunt Florry rolling a dresser on its little rollers along the hallway to the space at the top of the stairs that might have been the hotel's lobby.

"We met a man," Wendy said.

"A man! Where?"

At that moment they heard him coming down the main stairs. He was carrying a maroon-colored washstand.

"Hey!" Aunt Florry screeched, forgetting all about quiet. "That's mine! I was here first!"

The man set the washstand down, straightened his back, and caught his breath.

"There's more up there," he said peaceably.

"As good as that one?" She rushed over to inspect it. "I haven't had a chance to make a choice yet. Let me see the others before you take that one!"

Jason felt ready to sink into the floor. Wendy backed off down the hall out of sight, her hand over her mouth, her eyes bulging with laughter.

Aunt Florry stood belligerently at the head of the stairs to the street. "I want to see first what's left!" she repeated.

She reminded Jason of a feisty little dog. And about as stupid, he thought.

"Lady," the man said patiently, "I told you . . . there's more up there."

"Wait, then, till I have a look. Some of these are carved, and others are just plain oak."

"How can you tell under all that paint?" he asked, but she was already off up the stairs. He looked at the twins and shook his head. "Where'd you find her?"

"She's our aunt," Jason said gruffly.

"Better yours than mine," the man said. He picked up the washstand and started carefully down the last dark flight. "Happy hunting," he said over his shoulder.

"Isn't she something?" Wendy said, awed.

"She's brave," Jason had to admit. "He could have pushed her right down those stairs if he hadn't been so nice."

Aunt Florry prowled about the upper floor so long that the twins suspected she knew she'd lost the battle. When she came down, all she said was: "Imagine, grabbing that right out from under our noses!"

"There are other nice ones," Wendy soothed her.

They were willing to help carry one dresser home, but they found they really didn't know Aunt Florry.

She and Jason stumbled down the dark stairs with a large dresser. Wendy carried the drawers. Then Aunt Florry said that since the dresser had wheels, they could just as well lay a washstand on top of it and roll the whole thing down the street. Wendy must carry a kitchen chair in one hand and pull the shopping cart with the other. Aunt Florry filled the cart with a big tin box, a white enamel dishpan, three musty books, three restaurant soup plates, and two cups, black with dust.

Jason pushed the dresser, and Aunt Florry guided it. The tiny wheels caught in every crack; the washstand kept threatening to fall off. The few people who drove past watched curiously. Jason helped because he had promised, but he vowed never to get hooked again. He glanced back at Wendy. Her face was pink with embarrassment or effort, he couldn't tell which. Maybe she was just plain mad, as he was.

When they were finally riding up in the blessed privacy of their own elevator, Aunt Florry looked at her watch. "We have time to go back and get another dresser before supper."

"I have to cook," Jason said promptly. "What I'm planning takes a long time."

"I have to bring in the clothes," Wendy reminded her. "It's starting to sprinkle." It had never occurred to them that they might some day be grateful for their jobs.

"Rain?" Aunt Florry cried. "I must hurry! I'll take the hand truck and bring back at least one more washstand."

She stopped the elevator on the twins' floor. Dresser, washstand, and kitchen chair joined the collection along their wall.

After she had gone off, Jason stood in the middle of their part of the loft. It looked clean and cheerful compared to where they'd been. The plants helped, and Elf, and their books.

"This place isn't bad," he said.

Wendy turned from washing her hands. "If you don't mind living in a thrift shop! We were dumb to help her."

"But it was fun."

Wendy laughed. "You're as bad as she is." But he could tell that she'd enjoyed it, too. All except bringing things home.

Last Straw

AUNT FLORRY OWNED TWO HUGE GARBAGE CANS, BUT she never got around to putting them out. The animals ate the kitchen scraps. Gradually it had become more and more clear to the twins that she didn't throw anything away if she could avoid it, so Jason had offered to take the garbage down on Saturday mornings and bring the cans back up later, after the garbage truck had passed.

Once the routine was established, both Jason and Wendy got up early on Saturday and threw all the empty tin cans, bottles, and newspapers that Aunt Florry had saved all week into the cans. They had learned that once things were gone, she never missed them, but if she saw either of them throwing out an empty jar, for instance, she would claim she was saving it for some special use. Luckily, she liked to sleep late.

And gradually, Aunt Florry's apartment was beginning to look a little less messy, even though it was still crowded.

The Saturday morning after their trip to the old hotel they whisked around the kitchen, snatching an empty towel roll here and a sardine tin there, emptying wastebaskets. Wendy daringly threw away a stack of plastic berry boxes that had been gathering dust under a chair. Jason, not to be outdone, threw away seven egg cartons, each with the imprint of a different store. They jammed everything into the cans and put them and the laundry cart into the elevator.

They were meeting Tomas and going to Chinatown. There, they planned to buy Chinese pastry to eat in the park while the clothes were being washed.

Wendy snickered. "It's a good thing she never gets up early. Can you imagine if she ever looked in these? She'd scream!"

Jason grinned. "If that ever happens, we lose the game. By a thousand points."

Wendy pointed to one of the cans. "We forgot the lid."

"It doesn't matter."

But when they put the cans on the street, a puff of wind blew some papers off the top.

"I told you!" Wendy cried, scampering after them. Jason stuffed the rest deeper into the can.

Gathering pieces of paper, Wendy stopped to read one.

"Come on," Jason called. "We told Tomas ten o'clock."

"Hey, this is a letter!" Wendy said.

"You're not supposed to read people's letters!" he shouted.

"It's typed."

He had a feeling that didn't make any difference, but Wendy was saying, "Aunt Florry's requested to move by December 31st!"

Jason looked over her shoulder. They read the paragraphs together . . . something about applying for relocation and moving expenses. The twins looked at each other with raised eyebrows.

Tomas came running up, and they showed him the letter.

"Sure," he said, "that's the eviction. We don't get them anymore 'cause we know where we're going."

"Where?" Jason asked. He felt stunned. Tomas was the only friend they had . . . the only one who knew what a weird place they lived in.

"To the projects."

"When?"

"I don't know." He shrugged. "When an apartment comes up."

"Maybe Aunt Florry's moving there, too," Jason said hopefully.

"She said she wasn't. Before you came," Tomas told them.

They set out for Chinatown, still wondering what Aunt Florry intended to do.

"She acts as if she's moving in, not out," Wendy said. "Come back with us and see what our place looks like now. All week she's been bringing chests of drawers from that hotel." Wendy wrinkled her nose. "The whole room smells moldy."

"But she has to move!" Tomas said. "They're going to tear the building down."

"What about Luke?" Jason asked.

"He has to move, too."

"What if Aunt Florry won't?" Wendy suggested.

"They'll bring trucks and the sheriff, and move all your furniture to an old warehouse," Tomas warned. "Full of rats," he added.

"Oh," Wendy worried. "What would I do with Morgan la Fay?"

"And Elf and Goblin?" Jason added.

"What would you do with yourselves?" Tomas asked.

Wendy and Jason looked at each other. "I guess we'll have to go to Mother's uncle," Jason said. The thought made him feel odd.

They came to a huge cardboard box dumped on the sidewalk, with colorful scraps of fake fur spilling out of it. Tomas dived in without hesitation, and pulled out a long strip of furry green, winding it around his head. "Look!" he announced. "I'm a safari guide."

"How come it's here?" Jason asked him.

Tomas shrugged. "Some truck forgot it, I guess."

Wendy found a square of red plush. "Wouldn't this be pretty for Morgan!"

Jason plowed through trying to find a piece for Elf. He came across a long black strip that looked good for something, and then a triangle of blue. Wendy found two more pieces that struck her fancy. They tucked them into the shopping cart and started on.

"What if Aunt Florry sees this?" Wendy giggled. "She'll take the whole thing!"

Tomas laughed, but Jason hardly heard. He was making up his mind to ask Aunt Florry about the eviction.

When he did ask that evening, all she would say was: "We have plenty of time." He didn't like to say that they had found the letter, but he hated to think of what might be ahead. December made him think of Christmas. What would Christmas be like this year? He could think of only one word: Grim.

The very next day the weather turned cold. Jason got out of bed shivering. It was time they had some heat in their room. He looked at the gas heater first and wondered how to light it. Then, he opened the door of the potbellied stove and looked inside. He remembered using a stove just like it in the vacation cabin in Colorado. The summer evenings had been cold in the mountains, so his father had built roaring fires in the stove. Jason had been impressed, because while the stove heated the room it would also heat a kettle of water on top. It had burned a lot of wood; he remembered helping fetch it from piles kept near the cottage. He didn't see how you'd get wood around here.

When the twins went upstairs, to their surprise, Aunt Florry came out of her room wearing a robe and shivering. "Brrr!" she cried. "A real fall morning! Do you know how to cook oatmeal?"

The twins promptly said, "No."

"Oh. Well, get the box out and read the instructions, Jason, while I get dressed. Wendy, you set the table and find the raisins. Do you like raisins in oatmeal?"

"I don't like oatmeal," Wendy said. "Aunt Florry, can't we ever have eggs and bacon like other people?"

"What other people?" Aunt Florry asked. "Child, there are people in this world who have never heard of eggs and bacon." She went into her room and shut the door.

"She must be one of them!" Wendy grumbled, slamming bowls on the table.

"You didn't used to like eggs, either," Jason reminded her.

"I suppose you like oatmeal?" Wendy said, raising her voice.

"I *love* oatmeal," Jason said, which silenced her. He hated to start fights in the morning. It took him two hours to feel awake. Most mornings he fed the pigeons in a trance. He measured water and poured it into a pan, put in the raisins and set it to boil.

Aunt Florry bustled out of her room wearing blue jeans and a too-big sweater with holes in the elbows. It looked like something she might have found. She finished making the oatmeal.

"It's cold downstairs," Wendy said. She was certainly looking for a fight, but Aunt Florry didn't oblige her any more than Jason had.

"Yes, yes!" she said. "It's a good thing it's Sunday. I mean to get Luke to light the stoves right after breakfast, if he's there."

But she didn't go to ask; she sent Jason down instead.

"Tell her to light her own stupid stoves!" Luke growled.

"I guess she doesn't know how," Jason said.

"She knows how! If not, she ought to learn— Livin' in a loft for ten years. She knows how!"

Everybody was cross this morning, Jason thought. Maybe it was the cold.

"Okay," Luke relented. "I'll be up when I get dressed." He walked off toward the living end of his loft shaking his head. "She knows how! She's the greatest con merchant in the world, that's all."

Jason left, quietly shutting the door.

When Luke came up later, his usual good humor had returned. He brought a box of wooden matches and made Jason and Wendy both watch while he lit the pilot light on the gas heater. "Because these things go out sometimes," he said, "and you better know how to turn it back on."

"We could build a fire in the big stove," Jason said.

Luke snorted. "You'll be doing that anyway, come winter. You don't think this little heater will keep you warm, do you?"

The twins needed a moment for this information to sink in.

"Doesn't it?" Wendy said.

"Where do you get wood around here?" Jason scoffed. Luke was teasing them.

"Out on the street," Luke said, "from the cheese warehouses. You'll find it, if you get cold enough." He looked at all the furniture piled against the back wall.

"Maybe that's firewood," he suggested, making the twins laugh.

"All right," he said, "I'm going up and light Florry's now. If she hasn't got them so buried I can't find them."

They followed him upstairs. Aunt Florry had two heaters. He lit them both and winked at the twins when she thanked him. "It's no trouble," he said. "In fact, it's very easy. I could show you how this minute."

"But you've got them all lit, haven't you?"

"It's no trouble to turn them off and start over."

"Oh, no, no!" Aunt Florry protested. "I couldn't take up any more of your time. May I offer you a cup of coffee? Or a glass of wine?"

"No, thank you," Luke said. "Got to get back to my painting."

The twins followed him downstairs as far as their own door, hoping he would invite them on down to his studio, but he did not. They went disconsolately into their own room.

Wendy walked over to the bank of furniture and began poking through it. Then, she turned back to Jason with a look in her eye that foretold trouble. "We could burn *some* of it! This chair with three legs, for instance. She's never going to use that."

"You can't burn up somebody else's things."

"Oh, yeah?" Wendy said. "Just watch me. As soon as it gets really cold. I'm going to burn up this—and this nasty old table, and this—what's this? You know this place wouldn't be so bad, if it weren't for all this junk."

Jason came over to look. "That's the base from an old swivel chair. But you can't just burn it. It's not yours!"

"It's not hers, either! People left these things, and she picked them up, and now she's left them here, and we'll pick them up and use them to keep warm."

"Not me! At least not until we really have to," he conceded.

"Well, I will any old time!" Wendy moved over to the gas heater that was beginning to crackle as it expanded with heat. "Ugh! Oatmeal. And now we have to scrounge firewood."

Jason hoped that meant she wasn't really going to burn up Aunt Florry's furniture, at least not enough for Aunt Florry to notice. Besides, he was getting used to it. It made the place interesting.

"Just be glad that we have a roof over our heads," he said, "that they haven't torn the building down yet."

Wendy looked woebegone. "I can see us, trudging through the snow, shivering," she prophesied. "Keeping Morgan and Elf warm under our coats."

"Where are we going?" Jason asked, fascinated.

"To the orphanage," Wendy said bleakly.

"You know what I think?" Jason said that evening.

Wendy was lying on his bed, reading a book. He was at his desk dealing with math problems.

"I think we ought to write Daddy's lawyer. He might make Aunt Florry take us to live in a house. Or an apartment."

"Or we could go to Mother's uncle. After all, when December comes, we may be glad even for a . . . a chicken house," Wendy said.

"You can't just dump yourself on somebody. He might not want us. And besides, we don't know what it would be like. We . . . we're kind of used to this now."

Wendy saw the wisdom of that. "Okay!" she said, bouncing up. "Let's write Mr. Gibson! Tell him how crazy she is. Maybe he'll at least find out where she plans to move. That is *if* she plans to move."

"She has to," said Jason. "And that's just it. The next place could be a lot worse, unless she begins to look for something now."

Wendy hurried to get her notebook and pen. "Okay, what are we going to say?" she asked, sitting down at her own desk.

After some argument and crossing out, they achieved the following:

Dear Mr. Gibson,

How are you? We are not very fine. Aunt Florry is kind of strange, even for here. She makes us feed her pigeons and take the laundry to Chinatown for our allowance. We eat moldy cheese and oatmeal. (At school we have hot dogs, though, and hamburgers.) Then we take turns getting supper.

The reason we are writing to you is because Aunt Florry is supposed to move. It is called an eviction. We do not live in an apartment. It is called a loft. It is going to be cold pretty soon, and we have to go outside and look for wood.

Is there any way you could make her move into an apartment? Please write us in care of Mr. Tomas Lorca at the following address:

"We'll have to look and see what his address is," Jason said.

"And tell him to expect a letter," Wendy giggled, but Jason was frowning.

"If Mr. Gibson is still the newspaper's lawyer, he'd still be our lawyer, wouldn't he? Without Daddy?"

"I think so," Wendy said. "It won't hurt to try."

They mailed it that night.

For a week they talked about what he would write back, hoping every day an answer would come.

"I'll miss Tomas if we go West again," Wendy said one night. "And I never have gotten to the museum."

"Why go to a museum," Jason asked, "when you live in one?"

They looked at each other and laughed.

Accident

A FEW DAYS LATER WENDY ANSWERED THE DOORBELL and found Tomas with a letter. She ran upstairs with it, Tomas at her heels.

"It's here!" she panted, bounding across the room to where Jason was searching through his books for a Spanish paper.

"Well, open it," he advised.

The letter was typewritten, and looked very businesslike; but it started, "Dear Children." Tomas and Jason craned their necks and read it over Wendy's shoulder.

"He's coming here!" Wendy exclaimed.

"Not until December—"

"That's not long," Tomas said. "This is November."

"He says if the situation is desperate, we can phone him," Wendy pointed out. "Would you say we're desperate?"

"No," Jason said, "only worried."

"Me, too," she agreed.

Jason took the letter from her and read it again.

"So he'll come in December. That's okay," Tomas concluded. "She'll have a whole month to look for a place."

"We—" Jason was interrupted by a tremendous thud overhead, followed by the sound of things falling.

Tomas lifted his head. "What was that?"

"Just Aunt Florry banging around," Wendy said. "She's always dropping things."

"She dropped the refrigerator that time," Tomas said. They giggled.

Wendy referred again to the letter. "He didn't sound very friendly, did he?"

"It's a business letter," Jason told her.

"He could still sound friendly," Wendy maintained. "He's known us forever."

"Listen," Tomas said, lifting his head.

From upstairs came the sound of irregular tapping.

"Now what's she doing?" he asked.

"Sounds like she's trying to send a message," Jason said. "Maybe we ought to go see."

"Maybe something fell on her!" Wendy said. "Goodness knows there's plenty to fall."

They scampered upstairs. But at first, they saw no one in Aunt Florry's big room.

"Aunt Florry!" Jason called.

"Here! I—I can't get up."

She was lying on the floor in front of the open door of the closet storeroom. The stool and boxes lying at her feet told their own story. She had been standing on the stool, trying to take something from the top shelf, or put something back.

She was lying in the only clear space, surrounded by a rack of wire shelves stacked with paperback books, a magazine rack, a chair piled high with coats, a steamer trunk, a floor lamp, two shopping bags full of canned food, and a neat stack of shoe boxes.

Wendy knelt in the tiny space beside her. "Are you hurt, Aunt Florry?"

Aunt Florry closed her eyes. She looked pale. "I'm afraid I've broken my hip. I felt something snap."

Frightened, the children looked at one another.

"We'll call a doctor, Aunt Florry," Jason said, controlling the quiver in his voice.

"Yes," she said faintly. "Her name's in the little book. Dr. Schwartz. I don't dare move."

"I'll get a pillow," Wendy told her and scurried into the bedroom.

"Is there anything else I can do?" she asked, returning to slip the pillow under her aunt's head.

"I suppose I'll have to go to the hospital. You'll have to look after things here."

"Put a blanket over her, too," Jason called, while he waited for someone to answer the phone.

At last a woman's voice said, "Dr. Schwartz."

"I'm calling for my aunt, Florence Ward," Jason said. "She just fell. She thinks her hip might be broken."

The doctor sounded calm and brisk. "Tell her not to move. I'll send an ambulance right away. Give me your address please."

Jason told her.

"Is anyone there besides you?"

"My sister and a neighbor."

"All right. Tell Ms. Ward I'll meet her at the hospital. Meanwhile, get some things together for her—her pocketbook, a nightgown, and her glasses, if she wears them. All right? Any questions?"

"I guess not." He didn't have time to think of any.

"All right. Tell her not to worry. We'll have her up in a couple of weeks." She hung up.

Jason repeated the message to Aunt Florry. She replied with a groan. Wendy got Aunt Florry's things together and put them in a shopping bag. In no time someone was ringing the bell, and Tomas ran down to open the door.

Jason began moving grocery bags and boxes out of the way. Wendy helped.

"They can use the elevator, can't they?" she suggested.

"Yes! We can run it for them." He was glad she'd thought of it.

They heard men trampling on the stairs. Two white-jacketed attendants came in carrying a stretcher with wheels. They looked around the room. Then, as if all their calls were to the same kind of place, they began moving stuff out of the way to make room for the stretcher.

"Careful of the furniture, Al," the younger one said, and winked at Jason.

Jason felt better after that. Aunt Florry would be okay. Two weeks, the doctor had said.

Jason showed the men the elevator. They wheeled Aunt Florry into it. Riding down, she opened her eyes.

"Jason?"

"Here I am, Aunt Florry."

"Don't forget the pigeons."

"I won't." He felt like crying.

"There's no need for you to come along. If I don't call you, call the doctor tomorrow."

Wendy put the purse and the shopping bag beside Aunt Florry and kissed her cheek. "We'll come see you," she promised.

A few people had gathered on the sidewalk to watch her being rolled to the ambulance and slid in-side. The people began to leave as the men got in and shut the door. Jason read ST. VINCENT'S HOSPITAL on the side. The ambulance swung away from the curb, its siren making a low growl; it turned the corner and picked up speed.

The three who were left behind turned back to the elevator.

"How will she get along when she comes home? She won't be able to manage alone for a long time," Wendy said, as they were riding up. "I sort of wish we hadn't written that letter."

"Me, too," Jason muttered. "Mr. Gibson won't think it's so great if we're taking care of her. But somebody's got to."

As they got off at their floor, the building seemed lonesome and empty, even though everything looked the same. It was Jason's turn to get supper. He was glad to have something to do.

Tomas went home, and Wendy went with Jason to let the pigeons out, both of them rather quiet.

"It's going to seem funny," Wendy said at last.

"Yes," Jason agreed.

"We can get supper any time we like."

"We could anyway. She never set a time."

"Well, we can fix anything we like," Wendy said, adding, "I know, we could anyway."

"And don't say we can go to bed when we like," Jason told her, "because she never made us go to bed, either."

"Why were we so mad at her?" Wendy asked.

Jason shrugged. " 'Cause she's so crazy, I guess."

Wendy nodded. " 'Cause she made us work, too. But it's not so bad, really. At least we know what to do now."

The pigeons grew tired of aerial gymnastics and went in. The twins went downstairs.

"Let's go tell Luke," Wendy suggested. "He ought to be home by now."

Luke opened the door to their knock and invited them inside.

"Aunt Florry's in the hospital," Jason said.

"She thinks she broke her hip," Wendy added.

"No kidding!" Luke exclaimed. "Well! That's a stunner! When?"

"This afternoon," Jason told him. "We heard a thud and went upstairs, and there she was—on the floor."

Wendy said, "The ambulance came. With a stretcher and everything."

Luke draped himself on a stool and looked serious. "So you kids are all alone! No more Florry to bug you."

They grinned sheepishly.

"We're going to miss her," Jason admitted.

"Darn right you are!" Luke said. He frowned. "She'll be gone a few weeks, I wouldn't wonder."

"The doctor said she'd have her up in two weeks," Jason said.

"Yeah, but *up* don't mean recovered." Luke moved

across the room to look at the calendar. "We got a problem, 'cause I'm moving— The fifteenth. I got the place for sure this afternoon. I was going to tell Florry tonight."

Jason and Wendy gulped, absorbing this new information.

"What are we going to do with you? You can't stay here alone, can you?"

The twins looked at each other.

"Aunt Florry told us to look after things," Jason said.

"You smart enough to make out all right? Otherwise, I guess I could take you with me . . ." He rubbed his chin.

"She told us to look after things," Jason repeated. "We have to stay here."

"She wouldn't like us to leave," Wendy agreed. "She told us to look after the place . . . and the pigeons."

"Well, we got time," Luke told them. "Nearly a week. We'll talk to her before then."

The twins started upstairs.

"Let's ask him to supper," Wendy said on the way up.

Jason ran back down to invite him, but returned saying Luke had other plans; he would take a rain check.

Jason cooked, and Wendy washed the dishes. The

telephone didn't ring, though they brought their books upstairs and studied at the kitchen table, waiting for Aunt Florry to call.

"I guess we have to phone the doctor tomorrow," Wendy said at bedtime. "How soon can we call?"

"How about lunchtime?" Jason suggested. "Maybe afterward we can talk to Aunt Florry."

"Will you be scared to live here if both Aunt Florry and Luke are gone?" he asked when she was going into her bedroom.

"We won't be by ourselves," she said. "We have Goblin—"

"And Elf and Morgan la Fay." Jason laughed.

"And a loft full of pigeons!" Wendy shrieked.

The idea of pigeons being company kept them giggling long after Jason turned out the lights.

Alone

JASON WOKE UP REMEMBERING WHAT HAD HAP-
pened. He thought about it while he fed and watered
the pigeons. That done, he went down to Aunt
Florry's kitchen. He found Wendy there surveying
the disorder. Aunt Florry never swept the floor, and
neither had they; no one had dusted since the Sunday
they had gone to the Statue of Liberty.

"Tonight I'm going to try to straighten this place
up," Wendy announced. She giggled. "Aunt Florry
can't scream every time we move something, so maybe
we can get somewhere."

They ate breakfast and hurried off to school. Jason
found himself counting the hours till they could call
the doctor.

But at noon the nurse answered the phone. "Doctor
isn't in now," she said. "Can she call you?"

"I'm at school," Jason said indignantly.

"You'll have to call later," the nurse told him.

"After school," he reported to Wendy.

But after school they couldn't reach the doctor, either. They left their number with the nurse and took turns staying near the phone. Wendy tried to improve the room's appearance while Jason was up exercising the pigeons. She accomplished a little, but got very dirty. When Jason came down, she said, "It would be easier, if a person just knew what to *do* with all these things."

Jason shrugged. "You don't *do* anything with them," he said. "You just have them."

They both laughed, and then Jason went off to get his books so he could work on his homework while Wendy cooked.

The doctor didn't call. The twins went to bed feeling lonely.

Next day at noon they telephoned again. This time the office nurse gave them a message: The doctor would telephone that afternoon. It looked, Jason decided, as if it were going to be a week of waiting for phone calls.

The doctor did call at last. She told Jason that Aunt Florry did have a broken hip and she had been operated on. A pin had been put in her hip to hold the cracked bone together so it would knit quickly. "She has a phone in her room, and she'll be able to telephone you in a day or two. How are you and your sister doing? Are you all alone?"

"No," Jason said quickly, "the man downstairs looks after us."

"I don't know why I said that," he told Wendy later. "I guess I didn't want the doctor to make a fuss, that's all."

"Well, Luke would look after us, if we needed it," Wendy said loyally. "He said so."

The next afternoon they raced home to hear from Aunt Florry. Tomas came with them.

"I get to talk to her first," Wendy said. "You talked to the doctor."

While they waited in the kitchen, Wendy began pushing furniture around. Tomas helped.

"I always did want to really clean this place up," he said.

As it happened, it was the doorbell that rang. Jason ran downstairs. When he opened the door, a man with a briefcase confronted him.

"Good afternoon," the man said. "I'm from the City Bureau of Relocation." He consulted a list. "I'd like to speak to Ms. Ward."

Jason gulped. "She isn't here."

"Are you related to her?"

Jason explained that he was her nephew.

"Does she have any plans for moving?" the man

asked. "You know, there isn't much time left. Tell her she should be looking for a place." He took a paper from his briefcase and wrote his phone number on the top. "Give her this, please, and ask her to call me." He handed it to Jason. "She should phone as soon as possible if she wants help in relocating."

Jason nodded. "I don't think she does, but I'll tell her."

The man said good-bye and walked away.

"It was a man from the city," Jason told Wendy and Tomas when he got back upstairs. "He wants Aunt Florry to call him. I told him she wasn't here."

"Good," Tomas approved. "He's trying to scare you."

"Yeah, I know," Jason said. "But he said she'd better be looking for a place."

"I don't suppose he can do anything until Mr. Gibson comes," Wendy said. She giggled. "Tell him we have to wait for our lawyer."

Jason said, "You tell him."

"Well, I don't think we ought to tell *her*," Wendy said. "She can't go apartment hunting now."

Jason nodded. "But what if he comes back?"

Tomas shrugged. "Don't answer the door. You can look out the window and see who it is."

The twins stared at each other. Doorbells, like telephones, demanded to be answered. Yet it might be scary and fun not to.

They spent the evening at the kitchen table, but Aunt Florry did not call.

"Do you think she's all right?" Jason asked.

"The doctor said so," Wendy reminded him.

"She said Aunt Florry would call us in a day or so. I just hoped it would be tonight."

"I hope she calls tomorrow," Wendy said. "We have to go to the store pretty soon, and there's not much money."

The twins hurried home the next afternoon hoping to hear from Aunt Florry. Tomas came with them again, because Mrs. Malloy had told him to find out if she could do anything for Aunt Florry or for the twins.

This time, Aunt Florry did not disappoint them. When the phone rang, Wendy jumped up, crossed her fingers, and ran to answer it.

Aunt Florry evidently asked how they were. Wendy said, "We're okay. How about you?"

Jason got up and went to stand beside her. Aunt Florry, when well, had a voice you could hear through a brick wall. Sure enough, Wendy was holding the receiver away from her ear. Jason was able to hear both sides of the conversation.

"I guess I'm all right," Aunt Florry was saying. She didn't sound very chipper.

"We really miss you, Aunt Florry."

"Well, I can't talk long."

"Does it hurt much?"

"No— Not all the time. I don't know how long they're going to hold me here. If you have any trouble, ask Luke, or Mrs. Malloy."

"We're okay," Wendy repeated. "We need some money, though."

"Of course you do! Look in the jar on my dresser. You'll have to make it last—" Jason didn't hear the rest.

"Jason wants to talk, Aunt Florry . . . Okay, I'll tell him . . . Good-bye." She hung up. "Could you hear what she said?"

"Some of it. Why wouldn't she talk to me?"

"She was tired."

His disappointment must have shown in his face, for Wendy said, "Tomorrow will be your turn. Come on, let's look for the money."

Aunt Florry's dresser was covered with dusty jars and boxes. Wendy made her way to it, picking a path through chairs loaded with clothes.

"What does she want with all these clothes?" Jason asked.

Tomas, who had followed them, said, "She saves them for some charity."

"Meantime she wears them!" Jason said with a laugh, and then felt bad for laughing.

"That money must be someplace!" Wendy unscrewed lids and shuffled things about, opened and slammed drawers.

"How about that one?" Jason pointed to a flowered can on the floor.

Wendy picked it up, pulled off the lid, and sure enough, took out a roll of bills.

"Do you call that a jar?" she demanded. "Anyhow, let's go to the store."

"We better make this money last a long time," Jason cautioned. "And I guess I'll keep a list. You know how she is about money."

Wendy nodded, counting the bills. "Good idea. Forty, forty-five, fifty dollars."

They were coming upstairs from their trip to the grocery when Luke opened his door. "Did you hear from Florry? Come in and tell me about it. How about a soda?"

While he got out the sodas, they told him what little there was to tell.

"I guess you didn't get a chance to tell her I'm moving," Luke said.

Wendy shook her head.

Jason said, "If it's all right with you, we decided not to tell her. She might worry."

Luke laughed. "I haven't seen her worry much about you kids. Still—you might be right." He slapped his knee. "You *are* right! What good's it do to upset her?"

"None," Wendy said.

Luke shook his head. "I wish I didn't have to move, but I do. I can't let that place slip by."

"We'll be okay," Jason said. "So we won't tell her, right? Don't tell the doctor, either," he cautioned Wendy.

"Of course I won't," she said, insulted.

"You're good kids," Luke said. "Come on, I'll take you to Chinatown."

Dinner in Chinatown with Luke was the nicest thing that had happened to them in New York. The restaurant was in a basement, with tables crowded together. Luke ordered sweet and sour shrimp, chicken cooked with peanuts and ginger, and other strange dishes. He showed them how to eat with chopsticks, but they soon gave up and went back to forks.

"That was fun," Jason told him when they were walking back home. "Thank you."

"Call it a farewell party," Luke said.

It was. He began moving his belongings on Saturday. By Sunday night he was finished. The twins helped him carry the last load down to his car. He gave them his phone number and his new address and patted Jason on the shoulder.

"You call me—hear?—if you have any trouble."

They promised, and Luke got into his car and drove away.

They went back inside thoughtfully, carefully locking the door. Then, though it was late in the afternoon, Jason remembered he hadn't let the pigeons fly. So, he and Wendy sat on the roof and watched the birds wheeling over the vacant buildings. Now and then a car passed below in the street, but the area for blocks around seemed empty.

"It feels like Robinson Crusoe," Wendy said.

"It won't tomorrow," Jason reminded her. "The street will be full of trucks again and noisy as usual."

After supper they turned the television on loud. And sat at the kitchen table, trying not to notice that Aunt Florry wasn't there, too.

Prowler

THE NEXT WEEK KEPT THEM BUSY. THEY HAD BEEN convinced they had lots to do before; but then, Aunt Florry had taken her turn at cooking and washing dishes, and she usually bought the groceries, though one of the twins often had had to race to the store before it closed because Aunt Florry had forgotten bread, butter, or something else they could hardly do without.

Now they each had to cook or wash dishes every evening, and there was also the shopping to do. They formed the habit of stopping off at the grocery on the way home from school.

Wendy, at least, was also determined to clean up Aunt Florry's quarters. Tomas came over and helped her struggle with the mess beyond the kitchen area. They carried a small rack of clothes into her bedroom, and threw out four empty cartons and a stack of newspapers. They shoved a steamer trunk up against one cleared wall and stacked things on top of it. They carried an old television set down to Luke's empty studio. And Wendy spent a lot of time taking things off the tops of the other furniture so she could see what was underneath while Tomas swept the floor. When they finished, though, they felt they hadn't made much headway; at best the room looked neatly crowded.

"If only she didn't *keep* everything," Wendy groaned, and Tomas just grinned.

Jason and Wendy talked to Aunt Florry every day on the phone, so it wasn't like being completely alone. But they couldn't visit her.

"They don't allow children," she said. "And I don't feel up to fighting it."

"She must be sick," Wendy commented.

They read her the return addresses on all the mail that came, but other than that even the mail was allowed to wait till she got home.

"It's a good thing we've got so much to do," Wendy said one evening. "It keeps us from feeling so alone here."

"And I suppose it's a good thing Aunt Florry made us learn to cook," Jason said. He was masterfully scrambling eggs for supper. "If she hadn't—"

Wendy was making toast. "We could have eaten TV dinners."

Sometimes they did eat them, but they both had discovered you could tire of them pretty fast.

At last it was Friday afternoon. Luke had been gone for nearly a week. And they were walking home loaded with books and food for the weekend.

Wendy said, "You know that girl who's been riding the bus mornings? She's in my French class. The reason we don't see her coming home is because she baby-sits after school. She lives with her mother. They just moved here. And already she's got a job."

"You've got a job," Jason pointed out.

"I bet she gets paid more," Wendy said. "Anyhow, she lives in a loft, too, further down Greenwich Street. She gave me her phone number. If we have trouble with French, her mother will help us. She speaks French."

"How about Spanish?" Jason was taking Spanish.

They were standing on the corner across the street from their building, waiting for a truck to pass. Jason looked at Wendy inquiringly, but he didn't let her answer. Instead, he grabbed her wrist.

"Quick! Hide!" He pulled her into the doorway of a butter-and-egg warehouse.

"What is it?" Wendy demanded.

"That man from the city! He's just coming away

from our door. I hope he goes the other way!" Jason stepped out onto the sidewalk and peered around a parked truck. The man was walking away up the street, briefcase under his arm.

"Lucky we didn't come home the old way," he told Wendy. "We'd have walked right into him."

They found he had shoved a paper through their mail slot, and again he had written his phone number on it.

Upstairs they dumped their bags of groceries on the table so Jason could write down what they had bought. But before he began, he looked up at Wendy. "What if he finds out we live here alone?"

"How can he find out?"

"He might," Jason insisted, "if he comes snooping around all the time."

"We could tell Aunt Florry to call him— But you know how excited she gets," Wendy said.

Jason agreed. "We'll keep dodging him, that's all. She'll be home soon. It's been almost two weeks."

That evening when they went out to walk the dog, they passed the rubble-covered lot where the building with the terra-cotta carvings had stood. Part of the brick walls had gone to fill in the basement. Broken pieces of terra-cotta could still be seen among the jumbled bricks and chewed-up wood.

"Look!" Jason said. Someone had dumped two

shopping bags full of scrap lumber into the lot. "That would be good to burn!"

They let Goblin off his leash, trusting that nothing would happen to him and that he would follow them home. It was Friday night; all the businesses were closed; the workers had gone home; and the streets were empty of cars. Each twin carried a bulging shopping bag of wood up the stairs, not bothering with the elevator.

"Poof!" Wendy said, dropping her bag near the stove. "We're getting to be like Aunt Florry. She can't walk down the street without finding something."

"We'll be glad, when it gets cold," Jason said. "It won't be hard to keep the stove going if we can find wood this easily."

"We can find wood if we have to," Wendy said.

Wendy took the laundry to Chinatown on Saturday morning, even though Aunt Florry wasn't there to see. She took the sheets off the beds and planned to make up Aunt Florry's bed fresh and clean, to be ready for her homecoming.

Jason turned the pigeons out. While they were flying, he swept their loft, as well as he could. The dust got in his eyes and also made him sneeze. It was a horrible job; he wished he'd never started it.

But it was better to be doing something. The building felt empty when you were alone! He was so glad to hear Wendy coming up in the elevator with the wash that he went with her to the roof and helped hang the clothes.

Sunday became another lonely day. They went to see what Tomas was doing, but he wasn't home. He and his sister had gone to a movie, Mrs. Malloy told them. The twins walked around the block and back home.

"I wish I'd asked Tomas how to get to the dinosaurs," Wendy said. "We could've gone there."

"You should have."

The day dragged on. There was homework. And a little more cleaning on Aunt Florry's floor, and some on their own. And then, at last the phone rang.

"Aunt Florry!" Wendy shouted, running to get it.

"She's early," Jason said, looking at the clock. Aunt Florry usually called around six, after her supper.

The caller was not Aunt Florry. Jason couldn't figure out who it was from listening to Wendy's end of the conversation.

In a moment she turned to him. "It's Ann . . . that girl I was telling you about. She wants me to come now and stay for supper. Do you care?"

She looked so eager that Jason didn't have the heart to coax her not to go.

She hung up, bubbling with expectancy. "Ann's

doing her French. She said to bring mine, and we'd do it together. I've got mine done, but I can check it."

"That's nice." Jason tried not to sound forlorn.

"I can't wait to see their loft. I bet no place looks as crazy as this! Imagine, real food, cooked by somebody's mother!"

Something inside Jason twisted. A picture of his mother cooking in the kitchen rose before his eyes.

"Do you mind if I take Goblin?" Wendy asked. "So I can come back alone, after dark?"

"How long you going to stay?"

"I don't know. Not late. I'll come home after supper."

"Okay." Jason remembered a couple of good programs coming up on TV. "How do you know they like dogs?" he asked.

"She told me to bring him."

So, Wendy set out leading Goblin. "Next time I'll make her invite you, too," she called, going out the door. "Maybe we could invite her here . . . if she promised not to tell anyone we live by ourselves."

Jason sat at the kitchen table and watched TV. There was no other place to sit. During the commercials he finished up his homework. For supper he made himself a peanut-butter-and-raisin sandwich and ate it, wondering what Wendy was eating.

When Aunt Florry called, she had good news. She could walk a few steps, and she was going to a nursing home on Tuesday. She asked Jason and Wendy to stop at the hospital on their way to school and bring her a robe, her slippers, and a dress.

Jason promised and wrote down the things she wanted.

"Where's Wendy?" Aunt Florry asked.

Jason told her.

"You should have gone, too," she scolded.

"She didn't ask me," Jason explained patiently.

"She would have, if she'd known," Aunt Florry insisted. Then, with one of her swift changes of subject, "Have the pigeons been out today?"

"Yes. I did it this morning."

"All right. And water the plants. Don't forget." She hung up without saying good-bye.

How exasperating she was! Even when you talked to her only once a day. She might at least trust him! He hadn't once forgotten to fly the pigeons. She had never mentioned the ones she fed regularly in the little park. He guessed he was lucky not to be ordered to feed those. They must be surviving on bread, he thought with a grin.

Just to make sure the pigeons were all right, he went up to take a look. They seemed cozy and contented. Coming down, the corners of the hall were dark and gloomy. They made the place seem lonely and empty, which it was. To heck with the TV. His own area was better, more like home.

A wind was blowing up. In the stairway he could hear the loose iron shutter on the next building, squeaking and banging.

He turned on his reading light. The wind swooshed round the corner, rattling window sashes. Wendy ought to be home soon. He was glad he had a book to read so he could ignore the noises, but he felt a little amazed at himself because he wasn't scared.

However, when the noise was something upstairs hitting the floor in a series of bumps and thuds, he sat up with a start. For an instant he was frightened. Then he remembered. He had left Elf up there! She had probably toppled a stack of boxes. He had better bring her down before she broke something.

He laid his book down, crossed to the door, and went quietly up the stairs. If she thought he was coming to punish her, she would hide.

At the top of the stairs, a new sound brought him to a standstill. Somebody was walking across the floor!

He drew a sharp breath, his scalp pricking. His first thought was that Wendy had come home. But she wouldn't go upstairs first. She wouldn't play tricks, either. Besides, the footsteps weren't hers. He realized he was familiar with her tread. Had he locked the roof door? He couldn't remember. As he asked himself the question, he thought he heard the door bang in the wind. He listened, but heard only the rattling of windows. He was beginning to hope he was mistaken when the sound of steps came again. Stealthy now.

What should he do? The phone was in with the prowler. Oh, why had he left the door unlocked!

Instinct told him to get away, go downstairs, go outside, but Aunt Florry's door was opening. He froze. To run would be to draw attention. He stood still, hoping the dusk would hide him. The intruder might go the other way.

Eyes set in a face dark with whiskers peered round the door. They saw Jason, and gave a start of surprise. "Beg your pardon, sonny!" the man exclaimed. "I thought the building was empty." He shuffled briskly toward the upstairs steps and climbed them while Jason stood rooted to the spot. The sounds of footsteps went on up to the roof.

Jason sat down on the top step. He longed to rush up and lock the roof door, but he was still too scared. Elf put her head into the hall, saw him, and padded over, purring. He sat and hugged her.

At last his heart stopped pounding. So tucking Elf under one arm, he stole up and locked the roof door.

"It's my own fault," he told her. The man hadn't meant any harm. He had probably thought the building was empty until he saw the kitchen. Jason chuckled. Even if you saw the kitchen, you might think the place was a roomful of junk, unless you opened the refrigerator.

He peered into the room in much the same way the prowler had peered out of it. He could not have explained what made him hesitate to go in, but the room felt invaded. Some of the security had gone out of it.

He moved along the aisle, looking around to see what he had heard falling. There— Elf had knocked down Aunt Florry's stack of wooden cheeseboxes that served as spice shelves.

Then he saw the loaf of bread. He had just opened it earlier to make his sandwich. Now it was half gone. The man had meant no harm; he was just hungry. Jason was glad he'd taken some food.

He left the light on in the kitchen, but he took Elf down to his own floor, and as soon as he got inside, he slid the bolt.

"Why do you have this door locked?" Wendy asked when she came home and Jason let her and Goblin in.

"There was a bum in here."

"In here?" Wendy rolled her eyes around the room.

"Not here. Upstairs."

"Is he gone?"

"I scared him," Jason bragged. "He saw me and ran."

"You're kidding!"

"No, I'm not! I was down here and I heard something fall up there. I thought Elf had knocked something down. So I went up to get her. Then I heard someone walking."

Wendy shivered. "What did you do?"

"I was going to sneak back downstairs," Jason admitted, "but he came out and saw me."

"What then?"

Jason grinned. "I just stood there. But he was all right. He begged my pardon and said he thought the building was empty! Then he went back up to the roof."

Wendy looked apprehensively at the dark caves formed by the stacked furniture, as though something ominous might come crawling out.

Jason made a disgusted sound. "You know how he got in? I forgot to lock the roof."

Wendy's eyes widened. "What if he comes back?"

"I locked it now, silly."

"Hah!" Wendy said. *"Who's* silly?"

"Okay, I was," Jason admitted. "But I won't forget again, I promise you!"

"Did Aunt Florry call?"

"Yes. We have to take her some things tomorrow."

"Did you tell her?"

"Are you kidding? She'd have a fit! Actually, she called before it happened, but I wouldn't tell her anyway."

Wendy agreed to the wisdom of that. "Do we get to see her?" she asked.

"No. We have to leave the stuff at the desk. She said I should have gone with you to supper. I wished I had, boy, when I heard those footsteps!"

"I brought you something." Wendy began hunting in her coat. "Ann's mother sent a piece of cake." She hauled a paper-wrapped square out of her pocket. "She said she would have invited you if she'd known we were twins."

"That's what Aunt Florry said. She said we have to learn to speak up for ourselves."

The cake was yellow, with chocolate icing. Jason sank his teeth into it with pleasure. "What else did you have?" he asked, speaking through crumbs.

"Spaghetti and meatballs. Ann's mother looked over my French and it was right."

"What's her house like?"

"Like this, only not so full. Ann's mother knows lots of people who live in lofts."

"I'll bet none of them are as kooky as Aunt Florry, though," Jason said.

Wendy shrugged. "Ann's mother's a sculptor. Ann's coming over sometime." She sat quiet for a few moments. Then she said, "Jason, what if someone else gets in?"

"How can they? The door's locked now. Besides,

Goblin's here. You wouldn't let anybody in, would you, old beast?"

Goblin came to him, tongue lolling.

"I'm sorry I took him," Wendy said. "He should have been here."

"That's okay. Listen, you better hunt up Aunt Florry's things."

"What dress does she want? She's got about a million."

"So pick something out. Only not—" Jason giggled. "Not that one she wears backward!"

Wendy hesitated. "I don't want to go up alone."

"I'll go with you," Jason agreed. He hoped that when he returned to the kitchen with Wendy, the feeling that it was no longer safe would be gone.

While Wendy hunted for Aunt Florry's clothes, Jason restacked the cheeseboxes and replaced the spices. That done, the room seemed all right again.

"One thing about a lot of junk, the place seems cozier," Wendy said, coming out of Aunt Florry's bedroom. "Everything was so empty over there. I felt cold."

"It's crazy," Jason told her, "but it's ours." And it was. He had, after all, defended it against an intruder. Two intruders, if you counted the man from the city.

Blizzard

ON MONDAY MORNING, BY CONSTANTLY REMINDING each other, they remembered to take Aunt Florry's clothes. They got off the bus at 14th Street and walked to the hospital. A uniformed guard on duty at the desk took the package, made a note, and dismissed them. They walked on to school.

Jason said, "It's crazy going past the hospital every day and not being able to visit her."

"I don't think she wants us to," Wendy told him, a little breathlessly; they were walking fast in order not to be late.

"You know what I bet?" Jason was overcome by an idea. "I bet she's afraid someone would ask us questions! Like who was looking after us. If we said 'No one,' everything would get very complicated."

"I'll bet you're right," Wendy agreed.

That afternoon over the phone Aunt Florry told them they couldn't come to the nursing home, either. It was too far uptown—an hour's travel by subway.

Tomas confirmed that.

"At least she's not one of those grown-ups who complain you never visit them," Wendy said.

Aunt Florry called the next day from the nursing home. She sounded almost like her old self. She liked the place, though everyone was boorshwa. She had a wheelchair if she wanted to use it, and there were evening movies. She even asked Jason if he needed money. When he told her he had kept a list of what they had bought, she was pleased and laughed heartily. She promised to send them a check. The grocer would cash it for them, she said.

"Has anyone from the city been around?" she whispered through the phone.

Jason told her about both times—the first, when he had said his aunt wasn't home, and the second, when he and Wendy had hidden from the man.

"Good!" she chortled, forgetting to whisper. "Very good! Throwing people out! Because somebody at City Hall wants the property for something else. Good! Let them worry."

"Yes, but Aunt Florry—We've got to move sometime!"

"I refuse to be rushed. Here I am in a nursing home!

With a broken hip! What do they want from me?"

"If he catches us, what should I tell him?"

"Don't tell him anything! Oh! Oh! Here's the doctor! I'll call you tomorrow." She slammed down the receiver.

Jason walked away from the phone with his ear ringing.

"I'll be glad when I don't have to talk to her on the phone," he grumbled. "We better not let him catch us, that's all."

The rest of the week passed without mishap. Aunt Florry's check arrived in the mail. They cashed it at the grocery and paid themselves their allowance. Luke phoned to see how they were, and on Thursday Mrs. Malloy invited them to Thanksgiving dinner. With Tomas and his sister, Fernanda, they squeezed around the table in the Malloys' small, neat kitchen for large helpings of turkey, stuffing, and cranberry sauce. Mr. Malloy took his plate into the living room and watched a football game on television. This was the first time the twins had had a really good look at a New York apartment.

"We thought when we first came that everyone lived like Aunt Florry," Wendy said, making Mrs. Malloy laugh heartily.

They told Mrs. Malloy how Aunt Florry was having a good time at the nursing home, winning at Scrabble, seeing movies and meeting interesting people.

After dinner they went across the hall to Tomas and Fernanda's rooms and made a plan to go to the museum on Sunday. At last Wendy was to see the dinosaurs.

On Saturday morning at breakfast, Jason gave a sigh of satisfaction. "That man from the city didn't come around all week."

At that, the telephone rang. They jumped and stared at each other.

"It must be Tomas!" Jason exclaimed, getting up.

But it was Aunt Florry.

"Jason!" she cried. "They're predicting snow—a great deal of snow. Go to the store right away and lay in supplies. And fly the pigeons."

Jason glanced out of the window, and sure enough, the morning looked gray.

"Supplies?" he said vaguely. Did she think they were out in the country?

"Yes! Yes! Supplies! You sound half-asleep."

"I am."

"Well, listen. Let the pigeons out first. Then go to the grocery. Get bread and milk for three days. And look for wood on the way. It's liable to get cold, too."

"Bread, milk . . . wood," Jason repeated. Wendy came and stood beside him so she could hear.

"Is Wendy planning to take the laundry?" Aunt Florry asked.

"Are you?" Jason asked her.

Before she could answer, Aunt Florry was saying, "Tell her not to go. The clothes won't dry on the roof. She can help get wood instead."

"All right, Aunt Florry."

"Don't forget to buy food. You know our food comes from New Jersey and Long Island. And if the trucks can't get through—"

"Will we starve?"

"No, no! It's inconvenient, that's all. Make sure you have food for the animals. If it's not snowing after lunch, let the pigeons out again. Will you do that?"

"Yes, Aunt Florry."

"All right. Get busy now! Don't waste time. I have to go! They're starting Scrabble. Good-bye." She hung up.

Jason and Wendy went back to their breakfast.

"Did you hear what she said?" Jason asked.

"Yeah. We have to get milk, bread, and stuff, and more wood. How much wood?"

Jason shrugged. "All we can find, I guess."

Wendy stared out the window. "It probably won't snow."

"I hope it does!" Jason urged.

"Me, too. I wish we had our sleds."

Wendy wrote out a grocery list and cleaned up the breakfast things while Jason fed and flew the pigeons.

That done, the two took Goblin and the shopping cart and set out for the grocery. The sky—what they could see of it above the buildings—looked as gray and soft as mouse's fur.

At the grocery store other people apparently were preparing for snow, too. Not much bread remained, and only four containers of milk. The twins took two loaves and two quarts.

On the way home they found a stack of small, wooden boxes on a loading dock, awaiting the sanitation truck. The boxes said PRODUCT OF DENMARK on the side. Deciding they could easily be broken up for kindling, Jason carried two and Wendy carried one and pulled the cart.

But, the best place for wood turned out to be over on the other street, where the buildings were being demolished. The bulldozer had piled up a mountain of wood on one of the lots—flooring and window sash and panelling and broken furniture—all the timber of old buildings except the big beams. These were stacked to one side.

Around the edge of the mountain you could pick out pieces of every size. Jason found it exciting work. At any moment you might pull out a piece that would make half the pile collapse on you, or cut yourself on a rusty nail. Back home they would never have been allowed around such a place. One thing about Aunt Florry, she kind of trusted you not to be stupid.

Like she trusted you to cook without burning things. Well, no, that wasn't quite right. She burned things herself pretty often. But it wasn't such a big deal. The thing was—she didn't expect you to be perfect, like most grown-ups did. She did everything so badly herself that you couldn't help doing better!

Jason laughed to himself and went around the mountain to tell Wendy.

Wendy also had hauled out a stack of pieces small enough to go into the stove. They took what they could in the shopping cart and went home with the groceries. Then they went back for more wood. At the woodpile, they let Goblin off his leash. He trotted around smelling things, his red-brown tail waving like a triangular flag.

"That should be enough to last all winter," Jason said when they had made so many trips it wasn't fun anymore. They put the wood on the side of their room next to the old furniture, filling the crates they had found first with the pieces from the building site.

"It smells weird, do you notice?" Wendy asked, holding a piece to her nose.

"Like that hotel," Jason agreed.

"You know what I'm going to have for lunch?" Wendy asked on the way up to the kitchen. "Peanut butter and bananas on toast."

"I wish I had some more of that cake Ann's mother made," Jason said.

"Make one, why don't you?" Wendy said. "There's a cake mix in the cupboard."

"Sure," Jason said. "I'm studying to be a cook."

After lunch the snow had not begun to fall, but the radio kept promising it would. The twins went upstairs and let the pigeons out again. Not all chose to go.

"You'll be sorry," Jason told the lazy ones.

He went on up to the roof where Wendy had gone. He had begun to enjoy watching the pigeons fly. He knew some of them, too, by their markings. When Aunt Florry moved, what would become of the pigeons?

A feather drifted down, but no snowflakes.

When the pigeons had all returned to their loft, the twins went downstairs to spend the gloomy afternoon reading and doing homework.

"Listen to how quiet it is," Wendy said once, lifting her head from her book.

Jason listened. No sound at all could be heard except the ticking of the gas heater as the metal expanded.

"You know what it's like?" she said. "Like Navaho cliff dwellers, surrounded by cliffs, waiting for snow. We've got all our wood, food, and animals in our cliff house, too."

"Or we could be futuristic people," Jason suggested. "Somebody came from outer space and took everybody except us." He giggled. "We hid, but now we have to live in this big city all by ourselves."

"I'd rather be a cliff dweller," Wendy said.

Actually, that appealed to Jason, too, but he said critically, "There aren't enough trees."

"The country's too rocky for trees," Wendy stated, and put her nose back into her book.

Some time later a new sound drew Jason's attention. He raised his head to see white chunks of snowflakes plumping against the glass.

"It's snowing!" he screeched, rushing to the window.

Wendy joined him, and then Goblin got up and came to see what they were looking at. They watched for perhaps five minutes, during which time the flakes grew smaller, and when some fell on the brick ledge outside the window, they did not melt, as the first had done.

"That means it's getting colder, see?" Jason pointed out.

"Let's build the fire!"

"Pooh!" Jason said. "It's not cold yet! We have to make this wood last till the storm's over."

"I'm going to bring Morgan la Fay out then," Wendy said. "She's lonesome in my room."

Jason helped carry the rat's cage to a place beside Wendy's desk.

"Aren't you glad we've got all our supplies and animals in safe?" Wendy asked. "Did you ever see pictures of those big hairy mammoths? That's what's roving the streets out there . . . looking for something to devour."

"It won't be us!" Jason exulted.

They were drawn back to the windows by the snow, not in expectation of seeing a mammoth, but through the shifting white it was possible to imagine one, gray against the gray buildings, its curled tusks obscured only by the continuous fall of flakes.

Wendy turned away. "I'm going to make cocoa."

Jason continued to watch the snow, mesmerized, unable to turn his back on the window. By the time Wendy came back with the cocoa, snow had piled up on the fire escape, flake by flake, turning the cold black iron into black-and-white tracery. The empty windows across the street were marked with drifts of white.

Darkness descended early. Jason went around turning on lights. Then, as he put a record on the record player, he said, "How would you like to be really in a cave, with no lights, people, or anything?"

Wendy shivered. "I'm so bored," she said, "I'm positively glad it's my turn to get supper."

When they took Goblin for his evening walk before bedtime, it was still snowing. Enough had fallen to make it fun to run in, though it was too powdery for snowballs. It lighted the rows of dark buildings, picking out every ledge with a line of white, making a gray light everywhere, even though swirling flakes obscured the yellow streetlights.

Jason woke in the night to hear a blast of wind rattle the panes. He snuggled closer to Goblin and lay listening. The loose shutter was banging. That meant the wind had come up strong. A second later he heard it whirling snow against the glass. How good it felt to be safe—out of the wind and snow, and in his warm bed.

When he awoke again, clear gray light was streaming into the room. He looked toward the windows. It was *still* snowing! He bounded out of bed and ran to look out. The wind was blowing the snow off the fire escape as fast as the flakes tried to land. Wind was hurling snow in every direction. Across the street the drift around the doorway looked waist high.

He laughed in anticipation and ran into the bathroom to get dressed. Wendy, too, was awake. As Jason finished dressing she came out of her room, picking hair off her navy blue coat.

"One of those animals has been sleeping on this," she grumbled. "I can't tell which. They both have orange hair. I think it's Elf, though."

"You ought to hang it up," Jason said righteously.

"Yeah, like you do!" Wendy surveyed the collection of clothing gathering dust under his bed.

"Tomorrow!" Jason said. He called to Goblin, and they all danced out into the snow.

Not a car was to be seen and no tire tracks. In fact, the snow was blowing down out of the sky so fiercely that Jason had to keep blinking, and could scarcely see anything. Falling snow obscured the buildings half a block away.

Catching him off guard, Wendy pushed him into a snowdrift. When he tried to push her back, Goblin came bounding up, with the result that both of them were buried in white, with Goblin dancing around them and barking.

Laughing and snow covered, they tramped into Tomas's building and knocked on his door. He greeted them in pajamas, looking sleepy. "Come on outside!" Jason coaxed. Tomas shivered and said he was going back to bed. They asked to borrow his sled, but he didn't have one.

"That's funny," Wendy said, when they were back on the street.

Jason said, "What would we do with it, anyway? There aren't any hills to slide down."

"We could take turns pulling each other."

"That's for babies. Listen, let's go look at the wood-pile."

The dark, angular pile of broken lumber was being

turned into a white mound. "Like a big burned cake covered with icing," Jason said.

"You keep talking about cake," Wendy pointed out.

Jason nodded. "Maybe I will make one. Will you frost it?"

Wendy whooped at the idea and fainted into a snowdrift. Jason kicked snow into her face, making her shriek. That made Goblin jump at him again, barking. His forepaws caught Jason off balance and tumbled him into the drift beside Wendy.

She climbed out laughing, and then scolded Goblin for barking at them. "Next time we'll leave you home," she threatened. "Come on, let's go eat breakfast."

On the way she said, "If you make a cake, I guess I could make frosting."

They fried eggs for breakfast, and then made coffee to prove how grown-up they were.

After breakfast, Jason began the cake. First, he had to hunt for a pan of the size called for, among Aunt Florry's collection of tinware, which was stored in various cupboards. In looking through the cupboards, he came across a mixer, which was the only other thing he needed . . . besides eggs.

Aunt Florry called while he was in the midst of mixing the cake, and Wendy described what he was doing. Aunt Florry screeched that he must make her one when she came home.

Jason set the oven at the right temperature, put in the cake, and set the timer. Aunt Florry had bought the timer, she said, because she was always burning things, but one day she had left it too close to the fire and burned it. However, it still worked.

"That wasn't so hard," Jason said, licking the bowl. "Maybe I will make one for Aunt Florry the day she comes home."

They turned on the television. Bulletins kept interrupting the program to talk about the blizzard.

"I guess we won't be going to the museum," Wendy said.

Jason shrugged. "I wonder if Tomas is going to sleep all day."

They went upstairs together to feed and water the pigeons.

"I was wondering," Jason said. "What will she do with the pigeons when we move?"

"Leave them here, I hope."

Jason didn't answer.

Wendy looked at him. "Don't you want to leave them? Don't tell me you're getting to be a pigeon freak, too?"

"I like some of them," he admitted. "Look at that one over there, that very slim, white one with a little brown on it. I bet its mother or father came from a fancy breed."

Wendy shivered. "I wonder how they keep warm, poor things."

"Think of the ones outside!" Jason said. "Eating nothing but bread."

"Why don't you feed them, too?" Wendy said crossly. She was getting colder and colder.

"Why don't you take one apart and string its bones into a pigeon skeleton—you're so keen on bones? I'll bet Aunt Florry'd like that! You could give it to her for Christmas."

"Can you imagine!" Wendy exclaimed with a shocked grin. The idea was so outrageous she forgave him for beginning to like pigeons. They laughed all the way downstairs.

The hall and stairways had grown so cold they could see their breath, and they hurried into the comparatively warm kitchen.

"Hey, *smell* it!" Wendy cried, entering the room first. "It smells like real cake!"

"I nearly forgot about it," Jason confessed. "Good thing we didn't stay upstairs longer."

"That's the way our house used to smell. Remember?"

Jason did remember. For a while he almost wished he hadn't started the cake. But when the timer went *ding!* and he took the cake out, it looked so golden brown he felt too proud to be sad.

"It has to cool first before I can make the frosting," Wendy said, reading the box. "So, *now* can we build a fire?"

By the time they had started a fire in the wood stove, they were ready for lunch, so they let the fire die down again. After lunch, Wendy made chocolate frosting from the instructions on the box. Jason sat at the table and gave her the benefit of his experience and advice.

That finished, they discovered it had quit snowing, and they rushed outside for another romp.

"Dress warm!" Wendy mimicked, tramping down the stairs.

"That's one thing Aunt Florry doesn't do," Jason said. "She sure lets us wear what we please."

"We haven't had any colds, either—so far," Wendy added.

Outside not a footprint or tire track was to be seen. The sidewalks were lost under knee-high drifts. Even in the windswept street the snow was ankle-deep. They proceeded to walk up the middle of the street, Goblin trotting alongside.

"You'd think this was an empty city," Jason said.

"Do you feel lonesome?"

"A little," he admitted.

Their voices sounded brittle on the crisp air. Underfoot, the snow squeaked beneath their boots.

"What if we saw a mammoth's track now?" Wendy said.

"I'd go back to the house and call the police!" Jason said laughing. "Wouldn't they be surprised!"

At the corner they looked down the cross street and saw two firemen. They were shoveling snow away from the firehouse so the engine could get out, if called.

"It's nice to see some other human beings," Wendy admitted.

They walked around two blocks, looking at the new shapes the snow had made of familiar things.

"Let's call up Tomas," Jason suggested. "If he doesn't want to go to the museum, he can come over and eat cake."

"Sometimes I wonder if I'm *ever* going to see those animals," Wendy grumbled.

By the time Tomas arrived, the twins had rebuilt the wood fire.

"I could bring the television down," Jason said, but instead they sat around and ate cake and talked.

"This is nice!" Tomas said. "My sister and I used to live by ourselves, but it was summer."

Wendy started to question him, but was interrupted by the doorbell.

They looked at one another. "Who could that be?" Jason asked.

"Look out the window," Tomas said.

Jason moved cautiously across the room, as though the person outside might hear him walk. He peered down, but whoever was ringing was standing too close to the building to be seen from the window. Unthinkingly, he raised the sash and put his head out.

The sound of a window being raised must have been audible all down the silent street. The girl standing by the door heard and looked up.

"Oh, hi, Ann!" he shouted. "It's Ann," he said, pulling in his head and closing the window. "Go let her in."

A few minutes later she came into the room with Wendy. She was a small girl, with long, dark hair and gray eyes, pink-cheeked now and smelling of fresh, cold air.

"I was walking around in the snow," she said, "and decided to come see you. Isn't it gorgeous?"

Wendy and Jason agreed that it was.

"I bet there won't be school tomorrow," Tomas said.

"Oh, good-eee!" the girls squealed.

"So this is where you live?" Ann looked around the loft. "This is nice!"

Wendy took her to see her bedroom, and then upstairs to Aunt Florry's loft, and then on up to see the pigeons. When they came back down, Jason was cutting more cake. Ann and Tomas were very much impressed that he had made it.

"Hey, this is really nice!" Ann exclaimed again. "It must be fun with no one to tell you what to do."

Jason and Wendy admitted that it was, but Wendy

added in all fairness to Aunt Florry that even when she was home, she didn't boss them, as long as they did their jobs.

"Tell us about when you lived by yourself," Jason said to Tomas.

"It was two summers ago," Tomas said. "I was a lot younger then, and Fernanda and me, we were scared of Welfare. We lived with my father—see— in the same building where we live now; but he didn't come home for a long time. So I told Mrs. Malloy, who sort of looked after us even then, that we were going to our godmother's. Only we didn't have a godmother, so we moved into one of the empty buildings. You had to cross the roofs to get in. It was fun."

"Why did you move out?"

"I sprained my ankle. And then the cops found us. Only Barbara—she's an artist who used to live down the street—she and Mr. Malloy came with the cops. They fixed it so we could live with the Malloys."

Jason looked at Tomas with new respect.

"Hey," Tomas said, "I saw a Monopoly set when we cleaned upstairs. You know how to play Monopoly?"

Ann was willing, and the twins had always been told you should oblige your company, so Tomas unearthed the game. For two hours the four of them squabbled amicably over rents and mortgages. At the end of that time Tomas had most of the money, and everyone else was growing bored. Outside, the cold white afternoon was turning blue gray.

"Hey!" Wendy exclaimed. "Why don't you stay for supper? We'll have a party!"

"Yeah!" Jason seconded. "There's cake!"

"And there's chili," Wendy said. "We'll have chili, cake, and—and—applesauce."

Their guests got permission to stay, and approved the menu. Jason heated the chili upstairs and then brought the pot down and put it on the wood stove to keep hot while he and Tomas fetched bowls and spoons and crackers.

"This sure is nice!" Ann exclaimed again. "You're the luckiest kids I know."

"Do you think we're lucky?" Wendy asked Jason later, when Ann and Tomas had gone home.

"I suppose so," Jason said. "I mean, if Mother and Daddy had to get killed, I guess we're lucky to get to live with Aunt Florry. I mean—it's different. Nobody makes you do anything. We wouldn't even have to go to school very often if we didn't feel like it."

Wendy looked thoughtful. "I guess that's what scared us at first—not having any rules."

Jason nodded. "What are we going to do tomorrow, if there's no school?"

"Go to the museum! Ann knows how to get there, if Tomas doesn't want to go."

Mr. Gibson

NEXT DAY, AS TOMAS HAD PREDICTED, THE RADIO AN-
nounced that city schools were closed. The snowy
silence began to be shattered, however, by the sound
of snow shovels striking cement, tire chains striking
cobblestones, and the spinning wheels of trucks backing into snowdrifts.

The twins learned from Ann that the museum, too,
was closed; but the sun came out, so they played in
the snow. With Ann they built a snowman in an
empty lot, and her mother invited them both to supper. By Tuesday, however, they were ready to go back
to school.

On Tuesday afternoon they had gotten home and
were building a fire in the wood stove when the doorbell rang.

"That's not Tomas," Jason said. On the bus Tomas
had said he had lots of work to do.

"Then who is it?" Wendy asked.

Jason pressed his face against the window. "I can't see. Oh! It's a man with a briefcase. He's walking away!"

Ten minutes later, when they were upstairs eating after-school sandwiches, the phone rang.

Wendy went to it and then hesitated: "Maybe it's that man—"

"Aunt Florry isn't here, that's all," Jason said.

Wendy said hello, and then listened, looking surprised. "Yes, we're here," she said in a subdued voice. "Yes, of course . . . I guess we didn't hear the bell."

She hung up and looked at Jason with a scared expression. "That man wasn't from the city! It was Mr. Gibson!"

"Gosh!" Jason looked at the calendar. Sure enough, it was the first week in December.

"He's coming back," Wendy said.

Jason ran an eye over the kitchen. "Well, I guess it looks all right. I mean, there aren't any dirty dishes."

They went downstairs and quickly made their beds and picked up their clothes. While Jason changed the cat box, Wendy ran an eye over the room and picked up some balls of fur. Then they sat by the wood stove, awaiting his arrival.

"Well, he can't say it isn't like we said," Jason said, looking at the stove and the boxful of firewood that stood beside it.

"Aunt Florry was here at least, then."

"You think he's going to be mad?" Jason asked.

Wendy nodded. "He sounded mad. He said he couldn't believe he had the right building. That's why he went away and phoned."

"The thing is," Jason said, "it doesn't seem so bad now, does it?"

"No," Wendy agreed.

"As a matter of fact," Jason said, "I like it. And not just because Aunt Florry's gone, either. I'll bet not many kids get to build a fire in a wood stove. Or make a cake."

"Or have to sneak off to school," Wendy said, beginning to laugh. "We were so crazy! She didn't care! Why were we so scared of her?"

Before Jason could answer, the doorbell rang.

"You go," Wendy said.

"You talked to him. You go."

Wendy jumped to her feet. "Come on. We'll both go."

They ran down the stairs and opened the door. Mr. Gibson was standing in the snow, in galoshes and a black overcoat and a cattleman's hat. He was a tall man, who sometimes had joked with them and sometimes had paid them no attention at all. Now he was wearing a hearty smile, which faded as he looked at them.

"Well, well!" He shook Jason's hand. "Wendy—" He patted her arm.

Jason suddenly saw his sister through Mr. Gibson's eyes. With a shock he remembered how neat she had once looked. Now she was wearing unironed blue jeans, the same as he was, and neither of them had been paying much attention to whether their shirts were really wash and wear.

"We're *clean*," Wendy had said. "If it's freshly wrinkled, that shows it's been washed, doesn't it?"

She had taken off her boots when she got home, and now she stood shifting about in her thick stockings.

Jason thought he probably looked different, too. He knew he needed a haircut.

Mr. Gibson said, "I suppose you got my letter—"

Wendy said, "No," but Jason said, "Sure we did! *You* remember!"

"Oh, that one. I thought you meant recently."

"Come on upstairs," Jason invited, leading the way. Wendy locked the door and brought up the rear.

"So this is where you live!" Mr. Gibson said. "Boy, the halls are cold, aren't they! This isn't what they call a tenement, is it?"

"It's a loft building," Jason told him. "There used to be businesses here."

On the second floor, the lawyer stumbled over one of Aunt Florry's terra-cotta pieces. "Oh, uh!" he said. "I guess I'm suffering from snow blindness."

By unspoken agreement they took him into their own loft. With the plants, their furniture, and the stove giving off heat, it looked pretty cozy, Jason thought.

But Mr. Gibson stood with his hat in his hand, staring. "You mean you live *here?*" he demanded.

"Sure," Jason said, trying to sound off-hand.

Mr. Gibson exploded: "She calls this living quarters? This looks like an army barracks! Complete to the potbellied stove!" He walked into their living area, dumped his briefcase on Jason's bed, and surveyed the room. "On my affidavit! Florry must be insane."

Goblin came over and sniffed him to see what all the fuss was about.

"Won't you sit down?" Wendy asked politely.

He took off his hat and laid it on the bed, then sat on the edge of one of the prized office chairs and shook his head. "Well! You kids weren't exaggerating. What's that?" He pointed to the stacked furniture.

"That?" Jason echoed, stalling for time.

"Some antiques Aunt Florry's saving," Wendy said lightly.

"Where the heck does she sleep?" Mr. Gibson demanded. "Where's the kitchen?"

Jason explained that those rooms were on the floor above.

"What's that—the bathroom?" Mr. Gibson asked, getting up and going to inspect it. He pulled the chain that flushed the toilet and looked up as water rushed down from the wooden tank overhead.

"Tcha!" He turned back with a disgusted look and dusted his hands together.

"That's the first kind of toilet they made, practically," Wendy bragged. "It's an antique, too."

"I believe it! Where did you say Florry is?"

Jason said, "She's not here right now."

Mr. Gibson nodded. "Maybe you better show me the rest of the place."

"It's the same as this," Jason said. "The kitchen's here . . . and her bedroom upstairs is where Wendy's is, over there."

Mr. Gibson looked thoughtful. "Well, maybe I shouldn't look around without her permission. When did you say she's coming back?"

Jason shrugged. "I don't know, exactly."

"Will she be home to supper?"

"No," Wendy said.

His eyes narrowed. "Is she working nights?"

"No," Wendy said.

"Do you *know* where she is?"

"Yes," Wendy admitted.

Mr. Gibson sat down again and looked from Wendy to Jason. "Well—"

"She's in a nursing home," Jason said bluntly.

"*What?*" Mr. Gibson shouted. "Are you kids here alone?"

"We talk to her every day!" Wendy cried. "She tells us what to do, and we do it. Everybody says we're doing fine. Including Aunt Florry!"

Mr. Gibson shook his head. "She's just like she always was. I thought she'd gotten a little more sense after all these years. Who else is in the building? Anybody?"

Jason shook his head.

"There is, too!" Wendy objected. "There's a butter-and-egg business on the ground floor."

"What's she doing in a nursing home?" Mr. Gibson asked. "She belongs in a mental institution, if you ask me."

"She does not!" Jason cried, forgetting to be polite. "She broke her hip, that's why!"

Mr. Gibson said, "Oh! Sorry to hear that. All right, I'll go see her." He drummed his fingers on his knee. "I'll have to think what will be best to do with you."

"Do with us?" the twins echoed.

"Yes! You want to get out of here, don't you?" He looked around the room again. "All right—I better see the rest of this—this *pad!*"

The twins crept up the stairs in front of him like a pair of guilty mice.

"I wouldn't have believed it! I'll take my affidavit, I wouldn't have believed it." Mr. Gibson couldn't seem to stop shaking his head over the sight of the kitchen. "Where are those pigeons?" he asked, turning away at last.

So they had to take him on up and show him those, too.

"What are they?" he demanded. "What kind of pigeons are they?"

"Just pigeons," Jason said.

"You mean plain, old street pigeons?" Mr. Gibson said incredulously. "But nobody keeps those."

"Aunt Florry does."

"She's capable of anything," was Mr. Gibson's comment.

"Well, we like her!" Wendy said.

"Oh, I like her," Mr. Gibson hastened to assure them. "I like her well enough, but she's not fit to live with. You told me so yourself. And apparently she's not fit to look after you."

Jason and Wendy looked at each other. Neither knew what to say.

Mr. Gibson turned toward the stairs. "I've seen all I need to see. What your father would say, I don't care to think."

When they brought him back to his hat and briefcase, he said, "Say— How'd you two like to have dinner with me? Is there a restaurant around here?"

"A diner—" Wendy began.

"And an expensive place—where people come with chauffeurs," Jason added, and then, remembering their dinner with Luke, "and Chinatown!"

Mr. Gibson turned up his nose at Chinatown. "Let's take a look at the so-called expensive place. If they'll let us in," he added, thoughtfully. He glanced at his watch. "It's a little early, but I expect you youngsters could eat now? How have you been eating?"

"We take turns cooking," Wendy said with great dignity.

Mr. Gibson gave a disbelieving laugh.

The restaurant was dark and carpeted, its walls lined with dark, cracked-looking mirrors. The tablecloths were whiter than the snow outside.

"Now," said Mr. Gibson, when he had ordered their dinners, "I suppose the best thing will be to go and have a talk with Florry. If she's at a nursing home, I suppose there's no objection to children. It's not a hospital—"

"It's way up in the Bronx," Jason said.

Mr. Gibson gave a superior smile. "We'll have no trouble getting there. I'll let her know we're coming. What time do you get out of school?"

The twins told him, and he arranged to meet them the following afternoon.

They had asked for steak, which they hadn't had since coming to New York because Aunt Florry didn't believe in it. When their plates arrived, however, they found they weren't hungry. Jason wrapped most of the meat in his handkerchief to take home to Goblin. Mr. Gibson walked back with them to get Aunt

Florry's telephone number. They gave it to him, and he said he'd call her from his hotel.

Jason went downstairs with Mr. Gibson when he left, then came back into the room to find Wendy looking pale and disturbed.

"What are we going to do now?" she asked.

Which was just what Jason had been wondering. "Tell him we've changed our minds?"

Wendy frowned. "I don't think it'll do any good. What do you think he's planning to do with us?"

"He's not supposed to do anything with us," Jason said firmly. "We just asked him to make Aunt Florry move to an apartment—remember? Because we have to move and we didn't like this place. But now we do. Even so, she still has to move—"

"I think he's planning to do something with us," Wendy said, in an ominous tone that made Jason think of lonely towers or military schools.

"Well, we'll just tell him," Jason said. "We'll tell him we've changed our minds."

"He'll be mad. He doesn't think we ought to live like this. He's—he's boorshwa."

"Well, we'll tell him we want to," Jason repeated stoutly.

Only Goblin had any cause to appreciate Mr. Gibson.

A House

"HAVE YOU TOLD FLORRY WE'RE COMING?" MR. GIB-
son asked. He had met them after school, as arranged,
then hailed a taxi and gave the driver the name of the
nursing home and its address. It was as easy as that.
New York City was full of taxis.

"We haven't talked to her," Jason said. "Maybe she
called while we were at the restaurant. She usually
calls about six, and she doesn't like us to call *her*. Sometimes she's busy."

"Busy!" Mr. Gibson scoffed.

"Did you call her?" Wendy asked.

Mr. Gibson said, "Harrrumphf! No— I had some
other calls to make. Well . . . perhaps it will be as
well to simply confront her."

Jason took a deep breath. "What are you going to
tell her?" he asked.

"I'm going to tell her that that . . . loft or what-ever you call it is no place for you to live! It's no place for anybody to live! But Florry—thank Heaven —is not under my guardianship."

"Are you our guardian?"

"Yes, of course! I thought you knew. Well—that is —I'm one of them."

"Who's the other one?" Wendy asked.

"Your aunt," Mr. Gibson said shortly.

Wendy's face brightened.

"I'm going to tell her," Mr. Gibson continued, "I believe you should both go to boarding school—not a rigid one—one that takes, perhaps, both boys and girls. If she insists, would you mind spending your holidays with her?"

"We want to *stay* with her," Wendy said in a very small voice while Jason was still fumbling for words.

"Stay with her!" Mr. Gibson was all but shouting. "In that barracks? With pigeons . . . and rats?"

"There aren't any rats . . . except Wendy's," Jason objected.

"Pack rats!" Mr. Gibson snarled, meaning Aunt Florry. "How can children brought up in a lovely home, as you were, want to live in a—a—a junk shop! And dress like that? You wrote me you didn't like it." His eyes narrowed. He looked from one to the other of them. "What made you change your minds?"

"Well, there are lots of ways to live," Jason said

stoutly. "The way we used to live is okay if you have a mother and father, but the way we live now is good for New York. Anyway, for Aunt Florry. And we like her."

Mr. Gibson gave a nasty laugh. "I better get you away before you're as crazy as she is!"

"We just wanted her to get an apartment," Wendy said, still small-voiced.

Mr. Gibson tapped his fingers on his briefcase and looked out of the window.

When they drew up in front of the nursing home, Jason seized his last chance. "Are you going to tell her we wrote to you?"

"I don't know what I'm going to tell her," Mr. Gibson growled, and paid the driver.

They found Aunt Florry playing Scrabble with three other women. The twins were so glad to see her they forgot they were bringing the enemy. Wendy ran up and put her hands over Aunt Florry's eyes. Aunt Florry gasped, and then Wendy took her hands away and Aunt Florry saw Jason, and then Wendy. She screeched with delight, startling everyone in the big room. A passing nurse shook her head, but smiled.

Laughing merrily, Aunt Florry introduced the twins to her companions. "Bless you, my dears! How did you get here?" she demanded. Then she saw Mr.

Gibson, and her face sobered. "Oh, it's you," she said, as though to a jailer.

"Yes, Ms. Ward. I've come to have a talk with you."

Aunt Florry made a face and grumbled about interrupting her game. Jason noticed that one of the women had a lot of pennies and dimes laid out on the table. Were they playing Scrabble for money? No wonder Aunt Florry was enjoying herself so much. She must be winning.

They went into a little alcove and sat down. Aunt Florry walked carefully, with a slight limp, but she seemed to get around all right. She looked very rested, and Jason had never seen her curly hair look so neat. She was wearing a dress, too.

"I'm coming home Sunday," she said. "Is that what this fuss is about?"

"I'm glad you realize there's something to make a fuss about," Mr. Gibson began. "Florence, do you realize—"

He got no further. "Realize what?" she demanded, raising her voice. "That two youngsters the size of these can't look after themselves? Why—do *you* realize—that in the Middle Ages girls her age were married and having babies—"

Everybody at their end of the big sitting room must realize it now, Jason thought.

"And boys his age—" She pointed, "were in the

army, or midshipmen in the navy. Why, at his age one of his ancestors was fighting the Civil War!"

That ancestor had been fifteen, according to what Jason had heard.

"Who told you to come snooping?" Aunt Florry demanded.

A dark flush was stealing up Mr. Gibson's neck, but he kept his temper admirably and didn't betray the twins over the letter. "I had business in New York," he said. "As co-guardian, these youngsters are my business, too."

Aunt Florry surveyed the twins. "Do they look any the worse for wear?"

"They look like a pair of ragamuffins," Mr. Gibson said. "But healthy," he conceded before Aunt Florry could embarrass him again.

"Better ragamuffins than bourgeois brats!" Aunt Florry sneered.

Mr. Gibson sighed and backed down. "I understand your building's being torn down," he said. "Jason tells me you have until the thirty-first. The youngsters are worried about where they're going to live."

"I *told* you not to worry about that," she scolded Jason. "Of course I have a place! It was to be a surprise."

Jason and Wendy stared at her, feeling foolish. But it was so unlike Aunt Florry to plan ahead that they immediately shut their mouths and looked at each other. The look that passed between them meant, "Oh, yeah?"

Mr. Gibson believed her, because he was writing down the address. It was, she said, a big house on Staten Island. She had bought it a year ago.

"A house?" Wendy wailed. "A plain old house?"

"My tenants are moving the end of this month," Aunt Florry stated.

"Florry, you're supposed to be *out* by the end of the month," Mr. Gibson said despairingly.

Aunt Florry merely said, "Pooh!" She stood up carefully. "My Scrabble friends are waiting. It's been nice seeing you, children. We'll be back together next week, and we'll talk then."

Mr. Gibson rose and put his pencil back into his coat. "You don't mind if I drive out to see it, Florence?"

"I wish you would! Just remind the tenants that I have their security money—in case they've broken anything."

With a shake of his head, Mr. Gibson acknowledged he had lost that round.

But he hadn't given up. On the way home he said, "You might as well come with me tomorrow after school. What Florry calls a house may be anything from a silo to a roller rink."

Wendy's burst of laughter turned into a gasp when

Jason dug his elbow into her ribs. She clapped her hand over her mouth and gave him a penitent look.

Mr. Gibson let them out of the taxi in front of their building and looked at them unlovingly. "Do me a favor—comb your hair tomorrow, and see if you can't wear something clean!" He shut himself back into the cab.

"Boorshwa!" Jason said, looking distastefully after the taxi.

"Do you think she was telling the truth?" Wendy asked.

"I guess so. She must've been."

"Do you want to go back to living in an ordinary old house?"

"No." Jason had a momentary vision of wearing ironed shirts every day, and never having to do anything except be on time—getting up, school, meals, bed. If he could go back to living in a house with his mother and father, he would jump at the chance. But that couldn't be— So what was so special about a house and doing everything on time? "Maybe Mr. Gibson's right," he suggested hopefully. "Maybe it'll turn out to be a silo."

But when they arrived at the address the next day in Mr. Gibson's rented car, it was certainly a real house—big, white, three-stories high, with a porch all across the front.

"Is that it?" Jason asked in disbelief.

"That's the address she gave me," Mr. Gibson said.

"Can we go in?" Wendy asked.

"No. You kids stay here." He got out and went up onto the porch and knocked on the door.

"He doesn't believe her either," Wendy said, giggling with Tomas in the back seat. Mr. Gibson had allowed them to invite Tomas on the trip. Jason knew why: Mr. Gibson wanted to see what their friends were like.

"Look, there's some sheds in back," Jason said. "Maybe we can keep pigeons there—some really fancy ones."

They sat in the car and surveyed the neighborhood. The house stood at the end of a street of houses, all more or less in need of paint. The street itself was a spur off the highway at the edge of the community. Across the street, all the way to the highway and beyond, the landscape consisted of nothing but pale reeds, like gigantic wheat stalks. The reeds ended in a stretch of snowy flats that spread to the gray waters of the bay. Further down the highway Jason could see a high, snow-covered mound. Above it hundreds of gulls soared and dipped.

Tomas doubled up giggling.

"What's so funny?" Wendy demanded. When he

didn't answer, she ignored him. "Jason," she said, "you know what I'm going to do when we move here? I'm going to find a dead sea gull and string its bones together with wire, the way they do in museums. Aunt Florry won't care—if I use a sea gull."

"That's one thing you have to say about her," Jason stated. "She doesn't care what crazy thing we do—as long as we think it up ourselves."

Tomas had stopped laughing. "How will you get the meat off the bones?"

Wendy made a face, not having thought about that.

"Shhh!" Jason hissed. Mr. Gibson was returning.

Wendy's face cleared. "I'll ask our biology teacher!"

The lawyer came back to the car looking satisfied. Apparently, the woman who answered the door had verified Aunt Florry's ownership.

"It's sure on the edge of everything," he said, getting in, "but I guess you'll get plenty of fresh air. She says the school's nearby."

Mr. Gibson stopped at a gas station to inquire the way back to the ferry to Manhattan.

Wendy poked Jason, who was in the front seat, and pointed to a house next door to the station. She mouthed something. Jason could hardly see the house because the porch and yard were filled with furniture. His eyes fell on a white metal table, like a doctor's, iron bedsteads leaning against the clapboards, a bridge lamp, rocking chairs, and a lot of smaller things that had not yet emerged from their cover of snow. Next to the table stood a big, two-wheeled cart. A small, faded sign said, ANTIQUES—JUNK.

Tomas murmured something to Wendy, and Wendy fell into another fit of giggles.

On the ferry, Mr. Gibson kept telling them to stand back from the rail, as though they might fling themselves into the water. It seemed forever before he was letting them out on Greenwich Street.

Jason made bold to ask him if he thought the house was all right.

"I suppose so," he said grumpily, "if you want to live like that." He shook hands. "I'm flying back tomorrow, so I'll say good-bye now."

He drove off, and Jason heaved a sigh of relief. "Whew!" He turned to Wendy and Tomas. "What was so darn funny, anyway?"

They dissolved into giggles again. "That hill!" Wendy gasped. "Tomas whispered to me. It's the dump! That's why the sea gulls were there. And that other house—the one I showed you—I know—I just *know*—that's how Aunt Florry's is going to look! As soon as we live there a little while."

Jason understood what she meant. "As soon as she starts scrounging at the dump," he agreed, grinning ruefully.

"If Mr. Gibson had known!" Wendy said. "He'd just have fainted."

"Well, it's her house," Jason said. "I guess she's got a right to live the way she wants."

"Yeah." Tomas nodded. "Because that's the way she is."

"And if we want to live with her—" Jason began.

Wendy gave the kind of sigh she used to give over her dolls. "We'll just have to put up with her. She's all we have."

"You learn a lot," Jason said, "living with her. She makes things interesting."

"I told you she was okay, once you got used to her," Tomas reminded them. "I have to go. I have to clean the halls." He started toward home.

"And I have to cook supper," Jason said. He went upstairs, glad to be home, glad to be free of Mr. Gibson. Wendy, he knew, was as glad as he was.